"Nell, I miss you." James gazed at her warmly.

"James, we can't do this. *I* can't do this."

"What exactly is this?" he asked quietly. "The fact that we like each other but shouldn't?"

"*Ja*, we shouldn't," she said and started to turn away.

He captured her arm. "Nell, I'm sorry. I know I have no right to ask anything of you, but please…consider us being friends if we can't be anything more."

"I don't know if I can," she whispered.

"Why not?"

She nodded. "'Tis too risky. I want more but it will never happen. So I'm sorry, James, but we can't be friends. *Ever.*" Nell turned back to the buggy and climbed in.

Her eyes slid over him as they drove away. She was a fool for loving him, but she couldn't help herself. Her resolve hardened—she needed to find an Amish husband and soon, so that she could forget that the price to pay for following her heart could be detrimental to her future.

Rebecca Kertz was first introduced to the Amish when her husband took a job with an Amish construction crew. She enjoyed watching the Amish foreman's children at play and swapping recipes with his wife. Rebecca resides in Delaware with her husband and dog. She has a strong faith in God and feels blessed to have family nearby. Besides writing, she enjoys reading, doing crafts and visiting Lancaster County.

Books by Rebecca Kertz

Love Inspired

Women of Lancaster County

A Secret Amish Love

Lancaster County Weddings

Noah's Sweetheart
Jedidiah's Bride
A Wife for Jacob
Elijah and the Widow
Loving Isaac

Lancaster Courtships

The Amish Mother

A Secret
Amish Love

Rebecca Kertz

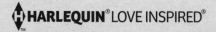

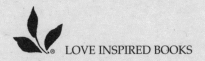

LOVE INSPIRED BOOKS

ISBN-13: 978-0-373-89938-8

A Secret Amish Love

www.Harlequin.com

Printed in U.S.A.

And now these three remain: faith, hope and love. But the greatest of these is love.
—*1 Corinthians* 13:13

For my mother-in-law—my other Mom—with love

Chapter One

Lancaster County, Pennsylvania

Nell Stoltzfus opened the door to Pierce Veterinary Clinic and gaped as she stepped inside. Pandemonium reigned in the crowded waiting room. Dogs growled and barked as they strained at their leashes. Some owners spoke sharply while others murmured soothingly as they struggled to control their pets.

A cat in a carrier situated on a woman's lap meowed loudly in angry protest of the ear-splitting canine activity. An Amish man sat in the corner of the room with a she-goat. The animal bent her head as she tried to eat a magazine in the rack on the floor near the man's feet. The goat was haltered, and her owner tugged up on the rope lead to keep her from chewing on the glossy pages. The animal bleated loudly as she stubbornly fought to eat.

The goat's noisy discontent joined in the cacophony of human and animal sounds as the unfamiliar Amish man glanced at Nell briefly before returning his attention to his goat.

She searched the room and frowned. Every available seat was taken. There was no sign of Michelle, Dr. Pierce's receptionist, whose job it was to check in patients and, on occasion, bring them into the exam rooms when the veterinary assistant, Janie, was busy.

Nell narrowed her gaze, assessing. On most days, there were usually two or three people in the waiting room. At least, every time she'd brought her dog, Jonas, in, there had been only a few people with their pets waiting.

During her first visit to Pierce Veterinary Clinic, just shy of a month after it opened, she'd sought medical help for Jonas after he was cruelly tossed out of a moving car. The visit had been a memorable one.

She'd met Dr. James Pierce, who'd refused to charge her for taking care of Jonas, requesting instead that she spread word of his clinic to anyone who might benefit from his services. And he'd startled her by offering her a temporary job as his assistant, based on her ability to calm her injured rescue dog who had lain trustingly in her arms.

"You have a natural affinity with animals, Nell," he'd told her during her first visit. During her second and last visit to the clinic, she'd declined but thanked him for his offer, even though she would have liked nothing more than to have the opportunity to learn more about caring for animals since it was her dream to minister to those within her Amish community. But her strong attraction to Dr. Pierce made it wise to keep her distance from him.

Today, Nell had been on her way home after a morning spent with her aunt Katie when she'd decided to stop at the clinic to purchase heartworm medicine for Jonas. At the veterinarian's suggestion, she had waited to ensure that her dog was fully healed before introducing the medication.

I should go, she thought as she gazed around the room. Clearly, she'd chosen the worst time to come.

She turned to leave, then glanced back when her attention was drawn toward the sound of a door opening and voices. A woman exited from a back room with a tiny kitten.

Nell waited patiently, expecting to glimpse Janie following closely behind. But it wasn't the assistant she saw. It was Dr. Pierce who escorted the woman to the front desk.

Nell watched as he sat at the desk and keyed something into the computer. She heard the deep, indecipherable rumble of his voice as he spoke. The woman handed him a credit card, and Nell continued to watch as Dr. Pierce handled the transaction, then gave the woman a receipt stapled to a paper that she knew would be the animal's health summary.

Nell froze, and her heart beat wildly as Dr. Pierce stood. She sent up a silent prayer that she would remain unnoticed, but she was powerless to move or to keep her gaze from checking for any changes in the man since she last saw him over a month ago.

She released a shuddering breath. The veterinarian was still as handsome as ever, dressed in his white lab coat over a blue shirt and black slacks. His short hair, which was a little longer on the top, was tousled as if he'd recently combed his fingers through the dark brown locks. His features were chiseled, his chin firm. There was sharp intelligence in his dark eyes. She recalled the brightness she'd first noticed in them, and his kindness and compassion when he'd treated Jonas. He had a gentle and sincere smile that warmed her all the way from her head to her toes each time she'd seen him.

A shiver of something pleasurable yet frightening slid down the length of her spine as she realized that she was attracted to him. Dr. Pierce still had the ability to affect her more than any other man since Michael, the man she'd loved and lost.

Nell stiffened and fought to banish the feelings. Dr. Pierce threatened her peace of mind. She drew a steadying breath as she struggled to pull herself together.

James. He'd told her at their first meeting to call him James. She shouldn't. But since that day, every time she saw him she immediately thought of him as James.

She closed her eyes briefly as she shifted farther into the corner of the room to stay unobtrusive. Nell swallowed hard. She didn't want the man to catch sight of her. As the eldest of five Stoltzfus sisters, she was expected to be the first to marry a faithful member of their Amish community. The last thing she needed was to fall for the English veterinarian. Being in James's company was dangerous. Even if he'd had feelings for her, there would have been no way for them to be anything other than polite acquaintances. Not that he felt the same attraction. It was all one-sided—her side.

The woman with the kitten turned to leave. On her way to the door, she walked past Nell, who froze. Nell knew that if she moved even a tiny bit, James might notice her.

Something shifted in his expression, as if

alarmed at the number of patients in the waiting room.

Nell waited for him to call back the next patient. As soon as he left, she would go. She'd return when Michelle was in the office. Jonas could wait another week to start his medicine. Or she could play it safe and go somewhere else and escape the frightening, forbidden feelings she felt any time she was near James.

She sighed. She couldn't go elsewhere. It wouldn't be right after all James had done for Jonas.

Nell remained still but then released a sharp breath when James suddenly saw her. They locked gazes. Surprise and pleasure flashed in the depths of his dark eyes, and she felt an infusion of warmth.

She recognized the panic in his gaze. She sighed. He was lost without his assistant, and she was the only one available who might be able to help.

She had a moment of revelation. *The Lord wants me to stay.*

"Dr. Pierce?" She stepped forward with a tentative smile on her face. Her heart beat rapidly as she remained the focus of his dark gaze. "May I have a word with you?"

"Of course, Nell." He waited for her approach.

"No help today?" she asked softly so that

the others within the room couldn't hear their conversation.

He shook his head. "Unfortunately, I'm alone today."

"I'll be happy to help if you'd like."

His eyes brightened as relief swept across his features. "I'd like that. Thank you."

James had never been happier to see Nell Stoltzfus. His receptionist, Michelle, was out sick, and Janie, his assistant, was on vacation, and he was swamped and alone dealing with a crowded waiting room.

As he'd watched Nell push out of the corner and approach, he'd been overcome with an immediate sense of calm. He'd never realized it before, but she had the same effect on him as she'd had on her injured rescue dog when she'd first brought Jonas in.

"Come into the back," he said, aware of the huskiness of his voice. He felt a jolt in his stomach as she smiled and followed him. Nell, a pretty young Amish woman, wore a spring-green dress with matching cape and apron. Her soft brown hair was covered by her white prayer *kapp*. Her nose was pert and perfectly formed, and her mouth was pink with a slight bow to her upper lip. He felt something shift inside him as he became the focus of her beautiful, brown gaze.

"Dr. Pierce, your waiting room seems unusually full." Her softly spoken words jerked him to awareness. She studied him with her head slightly tilted as if she were trying to gauge his thoughts. "I'd like to check your schedule."

They entered the reception area through a door off the hallway, and he showed her where to find the appointment book. "How long can you stay?"

"Through the afternoon." Her shy smile warmed him from the inside out. "May I use your phone?"

"Of course." She would need to get word to her family, he realized, so that they wouldn't worry about her absence. He waited while she made her phone call, trying not to listen as she explained the situation.

"*Ja*, Bob," he heard her say. "*Ja*, that would be *gut*. Thank you. Tell them that I shouldn't be too late." She glanced up to meet his gaze, and James instantly moved away to give her privacy.

He approached after Nell hung up the phone and stood. "Is everything all right?"

"*Ja*, 'tis fine." Her gaze met his, then slid away. He watched her study Michelle's appointment book. Her eyes narrowed. "You definitely don't have this many patients expected today," she murmured with a frown. "I'll have to do some rescheduling."

He started to leave, then turned. "Nell?"

She dragged her eyes away from the page to meet his gaze. *"Ja?"*

"Thank you." He spoke quietly so that no one would overhear him, but he knew immediately that she'd heard.

"You're *willkomm*," she breathed, and then she waved him away as she went back to studying the appointment book.

With a smile on his face, he opened the door to the back room.

"Dr. Pierce?"

He halted and faced her. "Yes?"

"Which exam rooms are available for patients?"

"One, three and four," he told her without hesitation. Then he entered the back of the clinic and went on to exam room two where his next patient waited.

James was examining the ear of a golden retriever when Nell knocked softly before opening the door.

"Dr. Pierce?"

"Yes, Nell?" he inquired without looking up.

"I've put Mrs. Rogan and Boots in exam room one and Mr. Jones with his dog Betsy in three. Mr. Yoder and his goat are in four. I rescheduled three patients for tomorrow because they didn't have appointments and your schedule could handle them then. Mrs. Pettyjohn is here with her poodle. She is your last appointment."

He straightened. "Already?" Amazed, he stared at her.

She gazed at him, her brown eyes filled with uncertainly. "Already?" she echoed.

"Are we really almost finished?" he asked. "Thank you for getting control of the situation so quickly." He looked sheepish. "I've been struggling about how to handle everyone for the last hour and a half." He rubbed his fingers through the dog's coat. "Bailey is going to be fine, Mrs. Martin."

The woman looked relieved as she glanced back and forth between them. "Thank you, Dr. Pierce."

"You're welcome." He turned toward Nell, pleased that she hadn't moved. "Nell, would you mind checking out Mrs. Martin and Bailey?"

"I'd be happy to," she said politely. She turned to the dog's owner. "Mrs. Martin, would you please follow me?"

James caught Nell's gaze as she waited for the woman and her dog to walk past her. He grinned in approval and was relieved to see her answering smile before she quickly followed Mrs. Martin.

Nell came into the back as he exited exam room two. "I forgot to tell you that Mrs. Rogan in exam room one had the next earliest appointment, then Mr. Jones, then Abraham Yoder."

He couldn't keep from studying her face. Nell Stoltzfus was genuinely lovely, with no need for artificial enhancement. He noted her smooth, unblemished skin, her pink lips, the reddish tinge to her cheeks. Since graduating from vet school, he'd had little time for a personal life, especially now that he was working hard to establish his new practice. He didn't know why, but there was something about her that made him long for something more. "Thank you, Nell."

"You're *willkomm*, Dr. Pierce."

He briefly met her gaze. "James, please," he invited. Again.

"James," she said then she blushed. "It was Mrs. Beggs, Mr. Merritt and Mrs. McDaniel whom I rescheduled."

"I appreciate your help," he told her, meaning it. "I didn't expect Michelle and Janie to both be out today. Janie asked for the week off, and Michelle is home with a stomach bug." He sighed. "I confess that I'm not good at juggling appointments."

Nell looked confused. "Juggling?"

He laughed. "Sorry, I'm not laughing at you but at myself. I don't know how Michelle does her job. She's good at what she does." He studied her thoughtfully, liking what he saw. "Apparently, you're good at it, too."

"At juggling appointments?" She arched her eyebrows.

"Yes." He chuckled, and the smile that came to Nell's pink lips had him mesmerized until he realized that he was staring. He stole one last glance at her as he opened the door to room one.

He heard her *"Ja"* before he closed the door.

The day passed quickly, and soon the last patient had been seen. Nell set aside the appointment book along with the checks, money and credit card transactions for the day. Fortunately, she'd quickly figured out how to use the credit card machine. She'd seen Bob Whittier of Whittier's Store use one often enough to recall how it was done.

She even had the opportunity to assist James with his last patient. Mrs. Pettyjohn's poodle, Roggs, had a lump above his right hind leg. James had determined it to be an abscess following a small injury. He'd asked for her help as he did minor surgery to open the wound.

"Will he be all right?" Nell asked as she handed him supplies and observed his work.

"He'll be fine. It looks as if he got into a rosebush. See this thorn?" He held up a tiny dark object that he'd removed with tweezers. "I'll prescribe an antibiotic for a couple of weeks. He'll have to wear a cone until his follow-up appointment."

Nell had enjoyed her afternoon at the clinic being his assistant. Too much. And she knew it had as much to do with the man as working with animals. Thankfully, the day was over, and after she helped to clean up, she'd be able to leave.

She cleaned the exam room floors with disinfectant. She was quiet as she mopped, her thoughts filled with what she'd seen and heard that day. When she was done, she emptied out the wash water and put away the bucket and mop.

"I'm finished with the floors, Doctor—James," she told him as he came into the reception area where she picked up her purse. "I'll be heading home now."

"Thank you so much for your help today," he said. "I don't know how I would have managed without you." He gazed at her a moment, then frowned. "Why did you come into the office today?"

"My dog, Jonas, is well and old enough to start his heartworm medicine."

"I'll get it for you." James retrieved a box from a cabinet and handed it to her. "Take it. No charge. If you come back tomorrow, I'll have cash for you."

"For what?" She frowned. "For helping out for a few hours? *Nay*, I'll not take your money."

"Nell…"

"*Nay*, James."

"But you'll take the medicine."

She opened her mouth to object but relented when she saw his expression. The man wasn't going to take no for an answer. *"Ja. Danki."* She gasped as she saw the time on the office wall clock. "I've got to go. *Mam* will be holding dinner for me." She hurried toward the door. "*Gut* night, James."

"Good night, Nell," he said softly.

Nell promptly left and ran toward her buggy, which was parked in the back lot several yards away from the building. She unhitched her mare, Daisy, then climbed into her vehicle.

As she reached for the reins, she watched as James headed toward his car. He stood by the driver's side and lifted a hand to wave. She nodded but didn't wave back. As she drove out onto the road, her thoughts turned to her family and most particularly her father, who wouldn't be pleased that she was late for supper.

She spurred Daisy into a quick trot and drove home in record time. As she steered the mare into the barnyard, her sister Leah came out of the house to greet her.

"*Dat*'s been wondering why you're late," Leah said as the two sisters walked toward the house.

"I was helping Dr. Pierce at the veterinary clinic." Nell stiffened. "Didn't Bob Whittier get word to you?"

"About a half hour ago."

"*Ach, nay,*" Nell said with dismay. "I didn't know he'd wait until that late. I called him hours ago."

"He sent word with Joshua Peachy but Joshua got sidetracked when he saw an accident on the stretch of road between Yoder's General Store and Eli's carriage shop. A truck hit a car and there were children..."

"I'm sorry to hear that. Is everyone all right?"

"Joshua didn't know."

"Is *Dat* angry with me?"

"*Nay*, Joshua told him what happened and why he couldn't get word to us earlier."

"But?"

"But he expected you sooner, and I don't think he was too happy that you stayed to help out James Pierce."

"Leah, you should have seen the waiting room. It was noisy and crowded, and there was no staff to help him. Both Michelle and Janie were out and he was alone. I believe that God wanted me to help him."

Her sister smiled. "Then that's what you tell *Dat*. He can't argue with the Lord."

As she entered the kitchen, Nell saw her other sisters seated at the table with her parents. She nodded to each of them then settled her gaze on her father. *"Dat,"* she said. "I'm sorry I'm late. I didn't expect to be gone so long."

To her surprise, her father nodded but didn't comment.

Nell took her place at the table, and *Dat* led them as they gave thanks to the Lord for their meal. Nell's sister Charlie started a conversation, and all of her sisters joined in as food was passed around.

As she reached for the bowl of mashed potatoes, Nell caught her *dat* studying her with a thoughtful expression. She felt suddenly uneasy. Her father might have seemed unaffected by her lateness, but she could tell that after supper he would want to talk with her, and she had no idea what he was going to say or how she would answer him. The truth was, she had enjoyed her afternoon at Pierce Veterinary Clinic too much to be sorry that she'd decided to stay.

"Tell him what you've just told me," her sister Leah had advised her.

I'll tell him how I felt...that God had wanted

me to stay and help James. Dr. James Pierce. She only hoped that *Dat* understood and accepted her decision as the right one.

Chapter Two

James admired the beautiful scenery as he drove his silver Lexus deeper into Lancaster County Amish country. Farmhouses surrounded by acres of corn dotted the landscape. Cows and sheep milled in pastures near Amish residences. Flowers bloomed in riotous color in gardens next to white front porches, while lawns were a splash of verdant green from the summer rains that had showered the earth recently. Familiar dark and solid-colored clothing flapped in the breeze, bringing back memories of James's teenage years living in an Amish community.

Seeing the Amish woman Nell again reminded him that it had been too long since he'd visited his mother and stepfather, so instead of going back to his apartment as he usually did, he turned in the opposite direction, toward the farm where he'd lived from the age of fifteen until he'd left

Lancaster County at eighteen to attend college in Ohio.

His stepfather and mother's farm loomed up ahead. The beauty of it nearly stole his breath even while he felt suddenly nervous.

He didn't know why. He knew they both would be glad to see him. It wouldn't matter to them that he'd moved into the area over two months ago and had stopped by only once. He'd set up his practice here because he'd wanted to be closer to his family. Yet, for some reason he'd stayed away.

He drove over the dirt road that led to his stepfather's farmhouse and pulled into the yard near the barn. He didn't see the family buggy. He parked out of the way of the barn door, in case whoever had taken out the vehicle returned.

There was no sign of anyone in the front or side yard as James turned off the engine and climbed out of his car. He paused a moment with the door open to stare at the house that had once been his home.

It had been hard moving into this house after his father had died and his mother had married Adam. It wasn't that he didn't want his mother to be happy. But he'd missed his dad. Grief-stricken, he'd been a terrible son, bitter and angry and difficult to control. But Adam was a kind man, who seemed to understand what James was going through. Because of Adam's understanding, patience and love, James had grown to love and respect his stepfather.

James shut the car door. He was here, and he would wait for everyone's return, not run like the frightened teenage boy he'd been when he'd first moved into Adam Troyer's house. He wandered toward the backyard and saw a woman taking laundry down from the clothesline.

"Mom?" He hurried in her direction.

She stiffened, then with a garment in her hand turned slowly. She was too young to be his mother although the resemblance to her was striking. His eyes widened. "Maggie?"

"Ja, bruder." Her mouth firmed. "You finally decided to pay us a visit."

It had been too long since he'd seen his younger sister. He felt a rush of gladness that quickly turned to hard-hitting guilt.

"You weren't home when I last visited." He regarded her with affection. "It's good to see you, Mags."

"Nobody calls me that but you." She dropped a garment into a wicker clothes basket.

He grinned. "Yes, I know."

Warmth entered her expression. "So you really did move back to Happiness."

"I did—close to two months ago." He held up his hand. "I know. I should have come again sooner. I've been struggling to grow my veterinary practice but…" He sighed. "It's no excuse."

He gazed at his little sister who was now a woman. He regretted missing her teenage years. He hadn't been here for her while she was growing up. He'd left home, driven to follow in his late father's footsteps. He'd attended college in Ohio, then went to Penn Vet for veterinary school. "I'm sorry I wasn't here for you."

She dismissed it with a wave of her hand. "I have a *gut* life. *Mam* and *Dat* are wonderful and Abby—" Her eyes widened. "Have you seen our little sister yet? You won't recognize Abigail, James. She's eighteen now."

Regret overwhelmed him, and James closed his eyes. "I missed too much."

"You're here now," she reminded him softly. She was quiet a moment as she studied him. "You'll have time to see her now."

"And Matt and Rosie?" he asked of his step-siblings.

Maggie smiled. "They are doing well. You wouldn't recognize them either." She studied him silently. "Matt is nineteen and Rosie's sixteen." She eyed him with curiosity. "Are you happy, James?"

Was he? No one had thought to ask whether or not he was content with his life—not even himself. He should be more than pleased with what he'd accomplished, but was he? He honestly didn't know.

"I enjoy helping animals, and my work reminds me of the time I spent with Dad. But happy? I'm working on it. What about you?"

A tiny smile came to her lips, and her green eyes sparkled. "*Ja*, I'm happy."

He stared at her, intrigued. He grinned. "You're being courted!"

She looked surprised and pleased that after all these years he still could read her so well. "*Ja*," she confessed. "His name is Joshua Fisher. He's a kind man."

"How old is Joshua Fisher?"

His sister narrowed her gaze at him. "Why?"

He didn't answer her.

She sighed. "He's twenty-one."

"I'm pleased for you, Maggie." Warmth filled him as he studied her. "You like the Amish way of life." Like him, she was raised English until their father died and their mother had brought them from Ohio to live in his grandparents' home in Lancaster County.

Her gaze slid over him. "You didn't seem to mind our Amish life," she reminded him. "Once you'd adjusted."

It was true. He had learned to appreciate the life he'd once rebelled against. The quiet peace that came from working on the farm when he was a boy eventually had soothed his inner turmoil over losing the father whom he'd loved, admired and always wanted to emulate.

"Where's *Mam*?" he said, slipping easily back into Pennsylvania Deitsch, considering how long he'd been away.

Maggie eyed him shrewdly. "In the *haus*." She paused. "*Dat*'s there, too."

"He's done working for the day?" His stepfather was a hardworking man, just like his own father had been. Would Adam scold him for staying away?

James experienced a sudden onset of uneasiness. The man who'd married his mother had been a good father to him, and he'd repaid him by being difficult and mean during those first months…and then he must have hurt Adam, leaving home when he did to follow the path he'd set out for himself away from their Amish village.

"*Ja*, you came at the right time. *Mam* and Abigail are making supper. Will you stay?"

He felt his tension leave him as he acknowledged the truth. "*Ja.*" He knew this was an open invitation. It was the Amish way to be hospitable and never turn a single soul away. "Will they be glad to see me?" he murmured. He studied the house. "I guess I'll head inside."

"James!" his sister called as he started toward the house. He stopped and faced her.

Maggie's gaze was filled with warmth and understanding. "'Tis *gut* to see you. Our *eldre* will be happy that you've come. Please, James, don't stay away too long again." She pretended to scowl. "I've missed your ugly face."

James couldn't stop the grin that came with the lightening of his spirit. "You'll be eager to get rid of me now that I'm living close and can visit frequently."

She shook her head. "*Nay*, I won't." She regarded him with affection. "I'll always be happy to see you, big *bruder*."

They eyed each other with warmth. "I'd better go," he said. "You'll be in soon?"

"A few moments more and I'll be done here."

"I'll see you inside then."

Despite anticipating a warm welcome, James felt his stomach burn as he crossed the yard toward the back door leading into his mother's kitchen. He drew a deep cleansing breath as he rapped on the wooden door frame.

The door swung open within seconds to reveal his stepfather, who blinked rapidly. "James?" Adam greeted softly as if he couldn't believe his eyes.

James offered a tentative smile. *"Hallo, Dat."* He watched with awe as happiness transformed his stepfather's expression.

"Come in!" he invited with a grin as he stepped

back to allow him entry. "Your *mudder* will be pleased to see you." He regarded James with affection. "I'm glad you've come back to visit." His eyes brightened as if Adam fought tears. "You look well, *soohn*. Your clinic is doing *gut*?"

James suddenly felt as if a big weight had been lifted off his shoulders as he entered the house. "It's doing better now, *Dat*." He needed this homecoming. Adam was still the warm, patient and kind man he'd always been, and James was so thankful for him. "It was hard to get started at first. I'm getting more patients, though."

Adam smiled. "I'm happy for you, James. I'm certain that you'll make a success of it." He gestured toward the kitchen table. "Sit, sit. I'll get your *mudder*."

James sat, aware that the house held all the wonderful cooking smells reminiscent of those he'd loved and remembered from his childhood.

Before Adam could leave to find her, his mother entered the kitchen from the front of the house. "I thought I heard voices, husband. Who—" Her eyes widened as they filled with tears of joy. "James!" She beamed at him. "You're back."

James grinned. "*Hallo, Mam*. I'm sorry I haven't been back sooner."

His mother brushed off his apology. "You're here now. That's all that matters." She met her husband's gaze with a pleased, loving smile. "He's come home again," she whispered huskily.

Adam moved to his wife's side and placed a loving hand on her shoulder. His smile for her was warm. "*Ja*, he has." He captured James's gaze. "And he is happy to be here." His stepfather grinned when James nodded. "I know 'tis near suppertime, Ruth, but why don't we have tea first?"

James watched his mother put on the teakettle. He had to stifle the urge to get up and help, knowing that it would upset her if he tried. In her mind, a woman's work was in the house while a man's work was on the farm or at his business. Adam's farm was small but large enough to provide for his family. His stepfather made quality outdoor furniture for a living, and Adam was good at his work.

The teakettle whistled as *Mam* got out cups, saucers and tea bags.

"It's *gut* to be back," James said sincerely. It was good to see his family and the farm.

He made a silent vow that he would return more frequently to spend time with the family he loved and missed, he realized, during the years he'd been away from Happiness, Pennsylvania.

Her father came into the room as Nell was drying the last of the supper dishes. "*Dochter,* when you're done, come out onto the porch. I want to talk with you."

"I'll be right out, *Dat*." She was putting away dishes when her sister pitched in to help. "*Danki*, Ellie." Nell hung up her wet tea towel on the rack when they were done.

"He'll not bite you," Ellie said softly.

Nell flashed her a look. "I didn't think he would."

"Then stop looking scared. *Dat* loves us." Her lips twitching, she teased, "Even you."

"I know, but I'm afraid he's angry that I didn't come right home from Aunt Katie's."

"He's not angry," Ellie assured her.

"Disappointed? Upset?"

"He was worried. Joshua didn't come until it was too late for him not to worry."

"I know. I'm sorry. I didn't know that Bob would send Joshua."

"Nor could you foresee the accident that would keep Joshua from getting to us sooner."

"Then why does he want to talk with me?"

Her sister shrugged. "Only one way to find out."

Nell nodded. "I guess I better go then."

She couldn't regret her afternoon at the clinic. She'd had a taste of what it might have been like if she'd accepted James's job offer as his assistant. She loved animals. She enjoyed spending time with them, caring for them, holding them. After her sister Meg became gravely ill, and Michael—the man she'd loved—had died, her animals had been Nell's only solace.

Working the afternoon at Pierce's Veterinary Clinic, she believed, was God's reward for doing the right thing.

Her father was standing on the front porch gazing at the horizon when Nell joined him.

"Dat?"

"Gut, you're here."

"Dat, if this is about today, I'm sorry that you were worried. I called Bob as soon as I knew that I'd be staying. I didn't know about Joshua and the accident."

"This isn't about today," he said, "although I was worried when you didn't come home."

"I'm sorry."

"You did what you should have. Joshua explained everything." He turned to stare out over the farm. "'Tis about something else. Something I've been meaning to talk with you about."

"What is it, *Dat*?"

"You're twenty-four, Nell. 'Tis time you were thinking of marrying and having a family of your own. Other community women your age are married with children, but you have shown no interest in having a husband. I'm afraid you're spending too much time with your animals."

Nell's heart lurched with fear. He'd talked previously of marriage to her but not negatively about her animals. "*Dat*, I enjoy them." She inhaled sharply. "You want me to get rid of them?"

He faced her. "*Nay, Dochter*, I know you care for those critters, and as unusual as that is, I wouldn't insist on taking anything away that gives you such joy. But having a husband and children should be more important. You're getting older, and your chances at marriage are dwindling. You need to find a husband and soon. If not, then I'll have to find one for you."

"How am I supposed to get a husband, *Dat*?" She'd loved Michael and hoped to marry him until he'd died of injuries from an automobile accident.

She knew she was expected to marry. It was the Amish way. But how was she to find a husband?

Chapter Three

Saturday morning found the five Stoltzfus sisters in the kitchen with their mother preparing food for the next day. This Sunday was Visiting Day, and the family would be spending it at the William Mast farm. Nell and her sister Leah were making schnitz pies made from dried apples for the gathering. *Mam* and Ellie were kneading bread that they would bake today and eat with cold cuts tomorrow evening after they returned home. Meg and their youngest sister, Charlie, were cutting watermelon, honeydew melons and cantaloupe for a fresh fruit salad.

"I'm going to Martha's on Monday," Meg announced as she cut fruit and placed it in a ceramic bowl. "We're planning to work on craft items for the Gordonville Mud Sale and Auction."

"What's so special about the Gordonville sale?" Charlie asked.

Ellie smirked. "She's hoping to see Reuben."

Meg blushed. "I don't know that he'll be there."

"But that's your hope," Nell said.

For as long as Nell could remember, Meg had harbored feelings for Reuben Miller, a young man from another Amish church community. She'd met him two years ago at their youth singing, after their cousin Eli had invited Reuben and his sister Rebecca, whom Eli liked at the time, to attend.

Reuben had struck up a conversation with Meg, and Meg immediately had taken a strong liking to him. Although the young man hadn't attended another singing, Meg continued to hold on to the hope that one day they'd meet again and he'd realize that she was the perfect girl for him.

Nell eyed her middle sister. "Meg, if you see Reuben and find out that he's courting someone, what are you going to do?"

Meg's features contorted. "I don't know," she whispered.

"You could be hurt, but still you won't give up…" Leah added.

Meg nodded. "I can't. Not if there is the slightest chance that he doesn't have a sweetheart. I know we spent only a few hours together, but I really liked him," she admitted quietly. "I still do."

"If you want a sweetheart, why not consider

Peter Zook?" Nell suggested, anticipating Meg's negative response.

"Peter!" her sister spat. "I don't want Peter Zook's attention."

"Peter's a nice boy," *Mam* said.

"Exactly! He's a boy." She sniffed. "Reuben is a man."

Nell held back a teasing retort. Peter was the same age as Reuben. He was a kind and compassionate young man who'd had the misfortune of falling in love with her sister, who wanted nothing to do with him. In her opinion, Meg could do no better than Peter Zook.

If only she could find someone her age who was kind, like Peter, to marry. An Amish friend she could respect and eventually regard fondly as they built a life together.

"I hope it works out for you, Meg," she said as she squeezed her sister's shoulder gently.

Meg smiled at her. *"Danki."*

"Would you and Martha like help on Monday? I can make pot holders for the sale," their youngest sister offered.

"That would be nice, Charlie," Meg said. *"Danki."*

The day passed quickly with the sisters chatting about many topics while they worked, including their Lapp cousins and who they expected to visit tomorrow at the Mast home.

Sunday morning arrived warm and sunny. At nine o'clock, their father brought the buggy close to the back door. The girls filed out of the house with food and into the buggy. Nell handed them the pies she and Leah had baked before climbing inside herself.

"*Dat, Onkel* Samuel and *Endie* Katie are coming, *ja*?" Leah asked as *Dat* steered the horse away from the house and onto the paved road.

"*Ja*, so your *onkel* said," he replied.

"*Endie* Katie said the same when I saw her the other day."

"Will all of our cousins be coming with their *kinner*? Noah and Rachel, Annie and Jacob, Jedidiah and Sarah?"

"I believe so," *Dat* said.

Nell smiled. She enjoyed spending time with her male cousins and their spouses. And she was eager to see Ellen, William and Josie's daughter, who had come to her aid and taken her and Jonas to the vet the day Nell had rescued him.

Buggies were parked on the lawn to the left in front of the barn when *Dat* pulled in next to the last vehicle.

Nell got out of the carriage first. Seeing her, Ellen Mast waved and hurried to meet her.

"*Hallo*, Nell! How's Jonas?"

"He's doing wonderfully. His leg is healed,

and he's gained weight. I'm about to start him on heartworm medicine."

The young blond woman looked pleased. "I'm so glad. I think it was a *gut* thing that you were the one to rescue him. I'm sure he's happy and well."

Nell beamed. "I'd like to think so." She and Ellen strolled toward the house as the other members of her family slowly followed.

Another gray family carriage parked next to theirs. "Look!" Charlie exclaimed. "'Tis the Adam Troyers!"

"Charlie!" Rosie Troyer called as she exited the vehicle. Abigail climbed out behind her and waved. The eldest sister, Maggie, and their brother Matthew followed and approached Ellen and the Stoltzfus sisters with a smile.

"I didn't expect to see you here," Ellie said with a smile. "I'm glad you could come."

"*Ja*, we thought our oldest *bruder* was coming also, but he was called out on an emergency," Maggie told them.

"*Hallo*, Ellen." Matthew turned to Nell next with a smile. "Nell, 'tis *gut* to see you."

Nell's lips curved. "Matthew."

Adam and Ruth Troyer approached. "Ellen, Nell. 'Tis *gut* to see you both. Ellen," Ruth said, "is your *mudder* inside?"

"*Ja*, I last saw her in the kitchen."

Loud, teasing male voices drew their attention. Nell's Lapp cousins Elijah, Jacob, Noah, Daniel and Joseph hurried out into the yard and gathered on the back lawn. Moments later, they were joined by her friend Ellen's younger brothers, Will and Elam.

Jedidiah came from the direction of the barn. "Found them!" he said, holding up a baseball bat and ball.

"Matthew! You going to play ball with us?" Isaac called.

"*Ja*, I'll play." With another smile in Nell's direction, the young man left to have fun with Nell's cousins.

"Nell, you watch the game and I'll bring your pies inside."

She smiled as she gave her pies to her friend. "*Danki*, Ellen."

Ellen entered the house, leaving her alone with Maggie.

"I didn't know you had another *bruder*, Maggie," Nell admitted, focusing on Maggie's revelation, as the baseball game began.

"*Ja*. He's a doctor and seven years older than me. He left our community when he was eighteen." Maggie's eyes filled with affection. "I've missed him so much. I was able to spend time with him yesterday but still…" She grinned. "Fortunately, he's moved closer to home, and we'll be able to see him more often. I'm sure you'll meet him eventually."

Nell didn't know why, but she felt an odd anticipation as if she were on the urge of learning something significant. "You said your *bruder* was called out on an emergency," she said. "What does he do?"

"He's a veterinarian. He's recently opened a clinic here in Happiness."

The strange sensation settled over Nell. Despite the difference in their last names, could James be Maggie's brother? If the young woman's sibling was a veterinarian, then she doubted that the man was a member of the Amish community. "What's his name?" she asked, although she had a feeling she knew.

"James Pierce." Maggie smiled. "He owns Pierce Veterinary Clinic. Have you heard of him?"

"*Ja.* In fact, 'twas your *bruder* who treated my dog, Jonas, after I found him."

"Then you've met him!" Maggie looked delighted. "Is he a *gut* veterinarian?"

Startled by this new knowledge of James, Nell could only nod at first. "He was wonderful with Jonas. He's a kind and compassionate man." She studied Maggie closely and recognized the family resemblance that she previously hadn't noticed between her and James. "How is he a Pierce and you a Troyer?"

"I am a Pierce." Maggie grinned. "Abigail is, too. But we don't go by the Pierce name. Adam is our stepfather, and he is our *dat* now. We were young when we lost our *vadder*. I was six, and Abigail was just a *bebe*. We lived in Ohio back then. After our *vadder* died, *Mam* moved us to Lancaster County where she was raised. She left Pennsylvania to marry *Dat* and start a life with him in Ohio. *Mam* was heartbroken when *Dat* died. She couldn't stay in Ohio without her husband and decided to return home to Lancaster County."

Maggie's eyes filled with sadness. "I didn't mind. I was too young to care, but James was thirteen and he had a hard time with the move. He loved and admired Dad, and he'd wanted to be a veterinarian like him since he was ten. James used to accompany Dad when he visited farmers to treat their animals. He was devastated by Dad's death, and he became more determined to follow in Dad's footsteps."

Nell felt her heart break for James, who must have suffered greatly after his father's death. "You chose the Amish life, but James chose a different path."

"And he's doing well," Maggie said. "My family is thrilled that he set up his practice in Happiness, because he wanted to be closer to us."

"He missed you," Nell said quietly.

The young woman grinned. "I guess he did. I certainly missed him. I'm glad to have my big *bruder* back."

Nell couldn't get what she'd learned about James and the Troyers out of her mind. It didn't help her churned-up emotions when, later that afternoon, James arrived to spend time with his family.

She recognized his silver car immediately as he drove into the barnyard and parked. Nell watched as he got out of his vehicle, straightened and closed the door. James stood a moment, his gaze searching, no doubt looking for family members. She couldn't move as he crossed the yard to where William Mast and others had set up tables and bench seats. They had enjoyed the midday meal, but there was still a table filled with delicious homemade desserts, including the schnitz pies that she and Leah had baked yesterday morning.

She couldn't tear her gaze away as James headed to the gathering of young people, including his sisters Maggie and Abigail as well as their stepsiblings, Rosie and Matthew.

Nell found it heartwarming to see that all of his siblings regarded him with the same depth of love and affection. She watched as James spoke briefly to Maggie, who grinned as Abigail, Rosie and Matthew approached him, clearly delighted that he'd handled his emergency then decided to come. She heard the siblings teasing and the ensuing laughter. Maggie said something to James as she gestured in Nell's direction.

James turned and saw her, and Nell froze. Her heart started to beat hard when he broke away from the group to approach her.

"Nell!" Warmed by the sight of her, James smiled as he reached her. "I didn't expect to see you here."

Her lips curved. "I didn't expect to see you here either."

"So you know my family." He didn't know why the knowledge startled him. Not that he was upset. In fact, it was nice to know that before they'd even met, he and Nell had shared an undiscovered connection.

"I've known them a long time. I had no idea that your family is the Troyers." She shifted her gaze to his sister Maggie. "Then I recognized the resemblance between you and Maggie." She smiled. "I've always liked your sister. She's a *gut* friend, and I like her sweetheart, Joshua Fisher, too."

"Joshua is here?" James attempted to pick him out of the gathering.

"*Nay.* He couldn't come today. His *grossmudder* is ill, and he thought it best to spend time with her and his family."

He was pleased to hear that Nell thought well of the man his sister loved. "He's a good man," he murmured, his gaze on his sister's smiling face.

"*Ja*, and he'll make Maggie a *gut* husband."

James settled his gaze on Nell's pretty, expressive features. "I'm glad you think so. I haven't met him yet, but I trust your judgment."

Nell appeared startled. She blushed as if embarrassed by his praise. "I'm sure you'll meet him soon."

They stood silently for several seconds. James felt comfortable with Nell, and she seemed to have relaxed around him, too.

"Nell."

She met his gaze.

"I was going to stop by your house. I received a phone call from Michelle today. Her stomach virus has spread to her husband and children, and she won't be back for days. Perhaps even a week. Janie isn't due back from vacation for another week. Would you consider working at the clinic next week? I'll pay you a good wage."

She seemed suddenly flustered, but he could tell that she liked the idea. "I'll have to ask my *dat*," she said.

"May I talk with him? I may be able to help ease his mind."

"I don't know…" She glanced toward an area

under a shade tree where a group of older Amish men were conversing.

"Are you afraid that he won't like me?"

"Nay!" she gasped, her eyes flashing toward his. She softened her tone. *"Nay.* It's not that."

"Then let me speak with him." He frowned. "Unless you don't want the job."

"I wouldn't mind working at the clinic again."

James grinned as he sensed the exact moment when Nell gave him permission to talk with her father.

He immediately knew who her father was when a man looked sharply at Nell and then him. "I'll be right back," James told her as he made his way to the man who'd left the group to approach.

"Sir," James greeted him. "I'm James Pierce. Your daughter helped me last Thursday at my veterinary clinic."

"Arlin Stoltzfus," the man said as he narrowed his gaze to take stock of James, "and I wonder how you know that Nell is my *dochter.*"

"A *gut* guess?" James said, slipping into Pennsylvania Deitsch and noting the man's surprise, which was quickly masked by a frown.

"What do you want, James Pierce?"

"A favor," James said. He softened his expression.

"What kind of favor?" The man eyed him with doubt.

"First, would you feel better knowing that I've come to visit my family—the Troyers—and not Nell?"

Something flickered in the man's expression. "You're Adam and Ruth's eldest son."

"*Ja*, I have the *gut* fortune to have their love."

The concern eased from Arlin's expression. "I'm sure you are a *gut* man, James Pierce."

"James," James invited, and Arlin smiled. "But now that I've seen Nell here today, I'd like to ask your permission for Nell to work in the clinic next week."

The man lowered his eyebrows. "Why?"

"I have no staff next week. My receptionist is taking care of her sick family as well as recuperating from illness herself. My assistant is away with her husband and not expected back until a week from tomorrow. I would need her to fill in for one week only."

Arlin glanced toward Nell, who was talking with two young women. "Have you mentioned this to her?"

James shifted uncomfortably. "*Ja*, I wished to know if she was interested before I came to you."

"And she is interested," the man murmured, "which is no surprise, considering how much she loves caring for animals."

Nell glanced in their direction, then quickly looked away, but not before James recognized longing in her expression. She wanted the opportunity to work in the clinic if only for a short time.

Nell's father sighed heavily as he studied his daughter. His expression was light, and there was amusement in his brown eyes as he met James's gaze. "She can work with you. She'll be disappointed if I refuse permission."

James smiled. "And above everything, you want your *dochter*'s happiness." He watched with stunned surprise as Arlin waved at his daughter to join them. Nell approached, looking fearful as she glimpsed her father's stern expression.

"You want to work for him?" he asked sharply.

"*Ja, Dat*, but only if you give permission."

Arlin's expression softened. "He belongs to the Troyers. I give permission," he said, surprising James.

James grinned. "Monday morning, eight o'clock sharp. Can you be there?"

"I can be there," Nell said. She turned toward her father. "I'll have my morning chores done before I go."

"*Ja*, I have no doubt of that," Arlin said.

"Do you need a ride?"

Arlin narrowed his gaze. "She will take the family buggy."

He nodded. *"Danki,"* he said.

"James!"

He glanced over and beamed as his mother approached. "I'm happy you could make it," she said.

He regarded her with affection. "I'm happy I'm here." His gaze flickered over Arlin and Nell who were standing next to him. "My staff is out, and Arlin has agreed to allow Nell to fill in for them next week."

His mother's eyes crinkled up at the corners. "You can rest easily with this one," she told Arlin. "He's a *gut soohn*."

James felt a momentary unease. He didn't feel like a good son. He'd left his family and his community to attend veterinary school and had little contact in the years that followed.

As if sensing his discomfort, his mother squeezed his arm. "He's moved back into the area to be closer to us," she said as she regarded him affectionately.

He did move to Lancaster to be close to his parents for he had missed his family greatly. The tension left him. Despite his past, he was determined that he would be a much better son and brother from this point forward.

Chapter Four

Monday morning, Nell steered her carriage down Old Philadelphia Pike toward Pierce Veterinary Clinic. She viewed the day with excitement. She'd learned a lot from just one day working with James. Imagine what she could learn in the next five!

When the clinic came into view, Nell felt a moment's dread. Learning from James was a benefit of working with the clinic, but working with the man could cause her complications she didn't need in her life. He was handsome and kind, but her attraction to him was wrong and forbidden.

Focus on what Dat *said.* Her father wanted her to marry. He'd find her a husband if she didn't find one on her own.

Nell knew that she just had to remember that although James had an Amish family, he was an *Englisher*. She couldn't allow herself to think of him as anything but her dog's veterinarian—and this week, as her employer.

When she pulled her buggy up to the hitching post in the back, Nell was surprised to see James's silver car parked near the back door. She'd arrived early. It was only seven thirty. She was sure she'd arrive before him and that she'd have to wait for him to show up.

She tied up Daisy, then went to ring the doorbell. Within seconds, the back door opened, revealing James Pierce dressed in a white shirt and jeans.

Nell stared and suddenly felt woozy. She swayed forward and put a hand out to catch herself on the door frame, but James reacted first by grabbing her arm to steady her. Seeing James looking so like Michael, her late beau, had stunned her.

"Nell?" he said with concern. "Are you all right?"

She inhaled deeply. "I'm fine." Like James, Michael, an *Englisher*, had favored button-down shirts and blue jeans. She'd met him in a grocery store before she'd joined the church and still had the option of choosing an English or Amish life. She'd chosen a life with Michael but she'd never had the chance to tell him before he died.

James still held her arm, and she could feel

the warmth of his touch on her skin below the short sleeve of her dress. "Are you sure you're all right?"

Nell managed to smile. "I'm well. *Danki*." She bit her lip. "Thank you," she corrected.

James let go and gestured for her to come inside. "Is the day getting warm?"

"A little." But the heat wasn't to blame for her wooziness.

"Come on in. I'll turn up the air conditioner so we'll be comfortable."

The impact of the man on her senses made her feel off-kilter. Nell blushed at her thoughts as she followed him into the procedure area. Fortunately, by the time James faced her, she had her feelings under control again.

"I'm glad you came," he said. "We have a serious case today. Mrs. Rogan is on her way in with Boots. Her Lab's eaten something—she's not sure what, but she believes he has an intestinal blockage."

"Ach, nay!" Nell breathed. "What will you do? Surgery?"

His handsome features were filled with concern. "I'll do X-rays first to see if I can tell where the blockage is."

"How can I help?"

He studied her intently. "Are you squeamish?"

She shook her head. "I don't think so. Did I seem squeamish yesterday? If you're worried that I'll faint at the sight of Boots's insides, don't be. I was in the room when my *mam* gave birth to Charlie, my youngest sister." She smiled slightly; the memory wasn't the most pleasant. "No one else was home."

He raised his eyebrows. "How old were you?" he asked.

"Nine."

He jerked in surprise. "You were only nine when you helped your mother deliver?"

"Ja." Nell's features softened. "I was scared. I can't say I wasn't, but once Charlie was born, I felt as if God had given us this wonderful new life. Charlie doesn't know that it wasn't the midwife who helped bring her into the world."

"Why not?"

"It's not important. What is important is that she is a healthy, wonderful young woman of fifteen."

She wondered if James was doing the math to realize that she was twenty-four. She saw him frown. Was he thinking that at the age of twenty-four most Amish women had husbands and at least one child, if not more?

"I'm glad you're not squeamish," he said. "Boots will be here any minute, and I'm going to need you by my side."

Even though she knew she shouldn't, Nell liked the sound of his words, of her and James working as a team.

After hearing Nell's story about delivering her youngest sister, James quickly did the math and was relieved to know her age. Then he frowned. Why did he care how old Nell was? It shouldn't matter as long as she did her job, which so far she'd been doing well. He wondered why Nell wasn't married.

Or was she? He'd never thought to ask. To do so now would seem…intrusive. He feared there was a story there, and one he wasn't about to ask her about.

James found he liked the thought of having her at his side while he did the surgery. And why wouldn't he, when after only one day she already had proved her worth?

"I'll be ready," she said. "I'll hand you the instruments you'll need. Maybe you can show me what they are now before Boots arrives? I don't want to hand you the wrong thing."

"Certainly." He moved toward the machine on the counter. There were several packaged sterile instruments in the cabinet above it. "This is an autoclave," he explained, gesturing toward the machine. "I put certain metal instruments in here to sterilize them."

She nodded. "What are those?" she asked of the two packets he'd taken from the cabinet shelf.

James proceeded to tell her what they were—a scalpel and clamps. Then he pulled out a tray of other types and sizes of the same instruments as well as others. "You don't have to be concerned," he said. "I'll pull out everything I need, and then I'll point to the instrument I want on the tray. You don't have to know all the names, although I imagine you'll learn a few as we use them."

He had just finished explaining the tools when he heard a commotion in the front room. "Boots is here," he announced. He was aware that Nell followed closely behind him as he went to greet the concerned woman and her chocolate Lab.

Nell helped him x-ray Boots while the dog's nervous owner sat in the waiting room. It turned out that Boots had swallowed a sock. After James relayed his diagnosis to Mrs. Rogan, he and Nell went to work. He encouraged Mrs. Rogan to go home, but the woman refused to leave until she knew that her dog was out of surgery and in recovery.

"Do you have other patients scheduled this morning?" Nell asked as she watched him put Boots under anesthesia.

"Fortunately, no. Not until this afternoon."

He readied his patient. "May I have a scalpel?" He gestured toward the appropriate instrument.

He needn't have bothered because Nell had already picked it up and handed it to him.

He smiled. "Perfect. Thanks."

She inclined her head, and they went back to the serious task at hand. It took just under an hour from the time they sedated the Lab until the time he was moved to recovery.

James went out to talk with Mrs. Rogan with Nell following. "Boots made out fine. We removed the sock, and there's been no permanent injury."

Edith Rogan shuddered out a sigh. "Thank goodness." She visibly relaxed as she glanced from him to Nell standing behind him. "Thank you. Thank you both."

"Boots may have to spend the night here," he said. "I'll keep a close eye on him today. If he does well, then you can take him home this evening. I'll call and let you know."

At that moment, the door opened and Mr. Rogan rushed in. "How is he?" he asked his wife.

"Fine," James said. "The surgery went well, but I'm afraid you may be one sock short."

The man shifted his attention from his wife to James. "You're Dr. Pierce?"

James nodded.

"Thank you, Dr. Pierce. Edith and I have grown very attached to him."

"He's our baby now that our children are married and on their own," Edith said.

"I understand," Nell said softly, surprising James. "I have a dog. I have several animals, in fact, and I would feel awful if anything ever happened to them."

Mr. Rogan studied her with curiosity. "You're Amish."

"I am?" Nell's brown gaze twinkled.

The man laughed. "Sorry. Sometimes I speak before I think."

"Well, you're right, Mr. Rogan. I am a member of the Amish church and community, and I had the privilege to work with Dr. Pierce during Boots's surgery." She paused. "He's a beautiful dog."

The man smiled. "That he is," he said.

"Edith, it's time for us to leave and let the doctor and his assistant get back to the business of saving lives and making our pets better."

"I'll call you later," James said as the couple headed to the door.

"I'll check on him often," Nell added.

The Rogans left, and suddenly James was alone with Nell. He was proud of the way she'd handled herself with Boots's owners, and he was pleased with how she'd assisted during Boots's surgery.

He glanced at his watch to see how much time he had before his first afternoon appointment.

"A successful surgery calls for a special lunch." He grinned. "Hoagies!"

She laughed. "Hoagies?"

"Sandwiches."

"*Ja*, that sounds *gut*," she said. "But I'll be bringing in lunch for us tomorrow."

"Sounds *gut* to me." James smiled. "We should check on Boots again before I order lunch."

After ensuring that the Lab was doing well, they ate lunch, then went back to work. The rest of the day occurred without any major incidents.

By the end of the afternoon, James was tired. When he glanced at Nell, he saw that she looked exhausted, as well.

"Time to call it quits," he said.

She nodded and reached for the mop and bucket.

He stayed her hand. "We can clean up in the morning." He eyed her with concern. "Are you all right?"

She blinked. "*Ja*, why wouldn't I be?"

"You've been quiet."

"Just thinking."

"About?

"Boots."

James smiled. "He's doing well. I'm glad I called the Rogans. They're happy to come for him. He'll do fine as long as they keep him still, leave his collar on and give him his pain medicine on time."

"And bring him back to see you on Tuesday," Nell added.

"Yes."

"Do you need me to do anything else before I leave?"

James shook his head. "No, go on home." He paused and couldn't help saying, "Be careful driving."

She nodded and left. James was slow to follow, but he watched her through an opening in the window blinds. Once her buggy was no longer visible, he took one last look around the clinic to make sure everything was as it should be, then he left, locking up as he went.

As he slipped onto his car's leather seats, he thought of Nell on the wooden seats in her buggy. He wondered how she'd react if she had the chance to ride in his car. There might be a time that he'd bring her home. He scowled. Probably not, because her time at the clinic was temporary, until Janie came back from vacation.

Nell was a fine assistant, he thought as he put the car in Reverse. She would manage fine until Janie's return.

A dangerous thought entered his mind, but he pushed it firmly aside. He quickly buried a sudden longing for something—or someone—else in his life other than his work, which had been the most important thing to him for some time.

* * *

Nell answered the phone when James's receptionist, Michelle, called into the office the next day. "Pierce Veterinary Clinic," she greeted. "How may I help you?"

The woman on the other end sounded dismayed. "Hello? This is Michelle. Who is this?"

"*Hallo*, Michelle. It's Nell. I'm helping James in the office until you or Janie returns."

"That's wonderful, Nell," the woman said. "I was worried about him managing the office alone." The two women chatted for several moments more, catching up, before breaking the connection. Nell went back to work, relieved that Michelle was glad to learn that she was filling in.

"Who was on the phone?" James asked as he came out to the front desk.

"It was Michelle. She and her son are feeling better, but now her husband and two daughters are sick."

"I'm sorry to hear that. Was she surprised that you answered the phone?"

"Surprised but pleased. She's been worried about you." She and Michelle had become friendly since Nell's first visit to the clinic.

James smiled. "I hope you told her to rest, recuperate and take care of her family."

"I did."

"Good."

Nell glanced at the appointment book on the desk. "Boots Rogan is due any minute for his follow-up."

"I want to check to make sure he hasn't bled through his dressing," James said.

Boots's appointment went well, and the owner took him home to continue the dog's recovery.

The afternoon went by quickly, and before they knew it, they'd seen the last appointment. But then an emergency call came in from Abram Peachy, a deacon in Nell's church district. Their mare Buddy had been injured by another horse.

James grabbed his medical bag. "Nell, will you come?"

"*Ja*, of course I'll come." Nell locked the front door and turned off the lights before she hastened through the back door and met James at his car. She hurried toward the passenger side and hesitated, uncomfortable being in such close quarters with James. He was suddenly there by her side, opening the door for her.

Feeling his presence keenly, she quietly thanked him, then slid onto the passenger seat. She ran her fingers over the smooth leather as James turned the ignition. The interior of the car smelled wonderful.

"Which way do I go?" he asked as he glanced her way.

She blushed under his regard and forced her

attention ahead. "Take a right out of the parking lot," she told him.

As he followed her directions, Nell was overly aware how close they were in the confines of James's car. Did he feel it too? The attraction between them? Charlotte was waiting outside for them as he drove close to the house. She hurried toward the vehicle as Nell and James climbed out of the car.

Her eyes widened and a look of relief passed over her features as she looked from James to Nell.

"What happened?" Nell asked.

"Something frightened Barney," Charlotte said. "Joshua was getting Buddy out of her stall when Barney reared up and came down hard against her side." She addressed James directly. "She's suffered a large gash. Can you help her?"

"I'll do what I can. Show me where you keep her."

Charlotte led the way, and Nell followed them to the barn where they found Abram near Buddy's stall.

Abram looked relieved to see them. "I put her back in her stall."

James studied the horse. "Good. She's in closed quarters." He addressed Abram. "I may need your help to hold her steady as Nell and I ready her to stitch up the wound."

"She's a gentle soul, but she's hurting bad," Abram said after agreeing to James's request.

Abram's son Nate entered the building. "Can you help us for a minute?" James asked after a quick look in the young man's direction. "Do you have any rope? We'll need to secure it to the rafters and around Buddy to help keep her steady after I give her a sedative."

"Ja," Abram said. "Nate, will you get that length of rope from the tack room?"

Nate immediately obeyed then slipped inside the stall, being careful to skirt the animal until he reached the front right side. *"Dat?* You *oll recht*?" he asked.

"I'm fine. Be careful, *soohn*," Abram warned as Nate came up on Buddy's opposite side.

James grabbed the rope and with a toss of his arm, he threw one end over the rafter until it fell in equal lengths to the ground. "Nate, could you wrap this around Buddy? Abram, you don't have a wench or pulley, do you?"

The man shook his head. "We'll make do."

He addressed Nell, "Would you get me a syringe and the bottle of anesthetic?"

Nell handed him the bottle and the needle.

He took it without looking at her. She could feel his concern for the animal. She'd seen different sides to the veterinarian over the past week, each more impressive than what she'd seen before.

His face was full of concentration as he inserted the needle. The animal jerked and kicked out, her hoof making contact with James's shin. He grimaced, but that was the only sign that he'd been hurt. Nell worried about him when he continued as if the horse hadn't clipped him.

He stood back. "We'll have to wait a moment or so until the anesthetic takes effect."

His eyes met Nell's. She gazed back at him in sympathy, recognizing pain in his face. She wanted to take a look at his leg and help him, but she remained silent. It was clear that he didn't want his injury to detract from helping Abram's horse.

She felt a rush of something she didn't want to feel. This man clearly loved animals as much as she did.

They waited for tense moments until the horse seemed to quiet. Nell looked at Abram. "It's *oll recht*," she said. She watched as he and Nate released their hold on the horse.

"You might want to leave," James said. "This won't be pleasant to watch."

The two men left, leaving Nell alone with James. He met her gaze. "All set?"

"Ja," she breathed, ready to do whatever he needed.

"Come around to this side. Bring my bag. I'll tell you what I need."

Nell watched while James worked on Buddy. He sutured the mare's wounds, noting how gentle he was with the animal, soothing her with a soft voice.

After twenty minutes, James seemed satisfied that he'd done all he could for the horse.

"Nell, would you please see if you can find a container of antibiotic? I'd like Abram to give her a dose twice a day. He can sprinkle it on her food."

Nell understood when she found the bottle and saw that the antibiotic was actually granules instead of pills.

Soon they were driving away from Abram's farm, heading back toward the clinic. Nell caught James's wince more than once as he drove, but she kept silent. She couldn't offer to drive him since she didn't know how and wouldn't be allowed anyway because of the rules in the *Ordnung.*

James pulled into the parking lot and drove around to the back as usual. She saw him grimace as he climbed out, but she didn't say anything as she followed him inside the building. James went into his office while she went right to work restocking his medical bag with the supplies he'd used at Abram's. When she was done, she entered his office and confronted him.

"You hurt your leg," she said. She swallowed hard. "May I see?"

He gazed at her a long moment, and she felt her face heat, but he finally nodded. Fortunately, the legs of his black slacks were loose. James gingerly pulled up his pants leg.

Nell gasped. His shin was swollen and severely bruised. She eyed the black-and-blue area with concern. "You should see a doctor," she suggested softly.

"I'll be fine," he said sharply. She didn't take offense for she knew he was hurting.

"I'll get some ice," she said and went into the kitchen.

When she returned, his head was tilted against the chair back, his eyes closed.

"James," she whispered. His eyes flashed open. She held up the ice pack. "For your leg."

"Thank you." He shifted, straightening. His pants had fallen back to cover his injured leg. He tugged up the fabric again, and Nell bent to place the pack on his bruised skin.

"It looks sore," she said with sympathy as she knelt to hold it in place.

James gave her a crooked smile. "A bit."

She shook her head, trying not to be uncomfortable looking up at him from near his feet. "You should go to the emergency room—or a clinic." She rose, and her gaze traveled around the room.

"What are you looking for?" James asked.

"Something to prop your leg up on so you can ice it properly."

"No need." He dropped his pant leg and rose. "It's time to head out. I can ice it at home."

Nell saw him wince as he moved, but she held her tongue. "I'll check the reception area and make sure it's locked up."

"Okay." He waited while she hurried out to the front room to lock up and retrieve her purse from under the desk. She took one last look around, then returned to where James waited near the back door.

"Thanks for your help today."

Nell shrugged. "That's what you pay me for."

A tiny smile formed on his lips. "I guess I do."

They headed outside together. James pulled the door shut behind them and made sure it was secure.

Nell saw that he held the ice pack and was glad. She became conscious of him beside her as she waited for him to turn. "I will see you on Wednesday?" she asked.

He hesitated. "Yes."

"Is anything wrong?" she asked, sensing a shift in his mood.

James opened and closed his mouth, as if to answer but thought better of it. "It's late."

Nell experienced a burning in her stomach. "*Ja*. I should head home." She turned away. Something was definitely bothering the man.

"See you in the morning, Nell."

She paused but didn't look back. She was afraid of what she'd see. "*Ja*, I'll see you then."

Then she hurried toward her buggy, feeling edgy and suddenly eager to be away and at home.

James watched Nell leave, then followed her buggy in his car until their paths split. He continued straight until he reached a small shopping center with a bakery, a candy shop and a small gift shop. He drove around to the back of the building, got out of his car and went in a back entrance that led to his apartment above the bakery.

As he started painfully up the stairs, he caught the scent of rich chocolate. Usually, he'd head into the bakery to buy whatever it was that Mattie Mast was making downstairs. But with his throbbing shin, the only thing he wanted to do right now was put ice on the injury.

The trek up the staircase was slow, and he stopped several times. He breathed a sigh of relief when he finally made it to the top.

His one-bedroom apartment was dark as he entered. He threw his keys onto the kitchen table and went to open a few windows to let in the day's breeze. The delicious scent of baking was stronger upstairs than down.

He refilled his ice bag, then, ignoring his rumbling stomach, he plopped down onto the sofa in his small living room, turned on the TV and shifted to put his feet onto the couch. He carefully set the ice pack that Nell had made on his swollen leg. He gazed at the television, but his thoughts were elsewhere.

It was Tuesday. There was still the rest of the week to get through. Would the pain in his leg let up enough for him to leave his apartment in the morning?

Nell will be there. He would make sure he got to work. She was helping him out, and he needed to be there.

Stretched out on his sofa, he stared at the ceiling with the sound of the television a dull buzz in his ears.

The ice felt good against his swollen leg. James closed his eyes, and the day played out in his mind. Nell's calming influence as she worked by his side. Their trip to the Amish farm, treating the mare. Nell's assistance with Abram Peachy and his son Nate. Her calming way with their mare Buddy. His growing friendship with Nell.

He saw Nell clearly in his mind—her soft brown hair, bright brown eyes and warm smile.

She'd worn a green dress with black apron today, with a white *kapp*, dark stockings and black shoes. He smiled. He wondered how she'd look at home when she was at ease, barefoot and laughing as she chased children about the yard, with sparkling eyes and her mouth curved upward in amusement.

James wondered how it would feel to spend time with her outside of the office.

His eyes flickered open as shock made him sit up. He was more than a little attracted to Nell Stoltzfus!

James shook his head. He had no right to think about Nell in that way. He scowled. She was a member of an Amish community, a community like the one he'd left of his own free will to choose a different path in life.

He forced his attention back to the television. He began to channel surf to find something— anything—that would consume his interest other than thoughts of Nell Stoltzfus.

Nell's four sisters were in the yard when she returned home.

"We heard what happened!" Charlie said.

"At Abram's," Ellie explained.

"Nate said you were both wonderful. He said you worked efficiently and quietly by the veterinarian's side," Charlie added.

"Was it true that James got kicked by Buddy?" Meg asked.

Nell studied her sisters with amusement. "Do you want me to answer any of you, or would you prefer to provide the answers yourself?"

Leah, the only sister who hadn't spoken yet, laughed. She was the next oldest after Nell. "How did it go?"

"Well," Nell said. "It went well. James sutured Buddy and left her in Abram's care."

"Was it awful?" Charlie asked. "Seeing all that blood?"

"I felt bad for Buddy, but I was *oll recht*. I didn't think much about anything but what I could do to help James."

The sisters walked toward the house as it was nearing suppertime. There would be work in the kitchen as they helped their mother to prepare the meal.

"Only three days more, *ja*?" Leah asked when their sisters had gone ahead into the house.

Nell faced her sister as they stood on the front porch. "*Ja*, in a way I'll be sad to see it end."

"But 'tis for the better that it will." Leah watched her carefully.

"*Ja.*" She leaned against the porch rail. "But until then, I'm learning so much. Things I'll be able to use in helping our friends and neighbors.

I know I can't take the place of a veterinarian but I'll be able to handle more than I could before."

Leah regarded her silently. "What's he like?"

"James?"

Her sister nodded. Her golden-blond hair, blue eyes and a warm smile made her the prettiest one of all of the sisters, at least in Nell's eyes. Today, she wore a light blue dress which emphasized her eyes. On her head she wore a matching blue kerchief and she was barefoot. She had come from working in their vegetable garden.

"You saw him at the Masts'," Nell reminded her.

"But seeing him isn't working with him."

For a moment, Nell got lost in her thoughts. "He's a caring man who's compassionate with animals. He's a *gut* vet. You should have seen him with Buddy. He—" She bit her lip.

"He was injured today," Leah said. "Nate stopped while you were gone. He said Buddy kicked him while he was trying to sedate her."

"*Ja*, but you wouldn't have known it by looking at him afterward. He worked as if nothing was bothering him when his leg must have hurt terribly." Nell had been amazed—not only by his skill but by his attention to Abram's mare.

"You like him."

"I wouldn't work for him if I didn't like and respect him."

"I know that, but I think you feel more for him."

"Nay," she denied quickly. "He's *gut* at what he does, and I respect that."

Leah nodded. As they entered the house, Nell wondered if her sister believed her.

She'd felt awful when she saw the extent of James's injury. She'd been startlingly aware of him as she'd pressed the ice pack against his shin. The sudden rush of feeling as she'd held the pack against his masculine leg for those brief moments had frightened her. Caring for him in that way had felt too intimate. She'd risen quickly and searched for a chair or stool to prop up his leg. When James had declared that it was time to go home, she'd been relieved.

"Nell," her mother greeted as she and Leah entered the kitchen. "I heard you had an eventful day."

Nell nodded. "It was more eventful for Abram's mare."

"She's all right?"

"Buddy's fine. James stitched her up as *gut* as new. She'll be in pain for a while, but he left Abram medication for her."

"Gut. Gut," Mam said. "Ellie, would you get the potato salad out of the refrigerator? Meg, you carry in the sweet and sour beans. Leah, would you mind getting your father? Supper is almost ready."

"What about me?" Charlie said.

Her mother smiled. "You can set the table with Nell."

Nell went to help her sister. She was home and felt less conflicted in this world she knew so well.

She might have imagined the strange tension between her and James. Tomorrow she'd put things in perspective and realize that the tenseness between them was just a figment of her imagination.

Chapter Five

Wednesday morning, Nell got up extra early to make her favorite contribution of potato salad for Aunt Katie's quilting bee. By the time her mother and siblings had entered the kitchen, she had finished cleaning the dishes she'd used. She automatically started to pull out the ingredients for the cake and pie that she knew that her mother wanted to bring.

"You're up early," Leah said.

"*Ja*, I thought I'd take a look at Buddy this morning before I head to the clinic."

"That's a fine idea," *Mam* said as she came into the room. "I'm sure Abram will appreciate it."

Nell ate breakfast with her family, then stayed long enough to clean up before she got ready to leave. She ran upstairs to get her black shoes. When she was done, she hurried downstairs to the barnyard. She chose to take the family pony cart and hitched up Daisy before she headed toward Abram Peachy's place.

She wondered what time James would arrive at the office this morning. Would she be able to reach him if Buddy suddenly needed additional medical care?

It was six thirty. She knew that Abram and his family most likely would be up and doing morning chores. No doubt Charlotte was already in the kitchen preparing food for this afternoon's quilting gathering.

The weather was lovely. Nell appreciated the colors and scents of summer. A bird chirped as it flew across the road and landed in a tree. The trees and lawns were a lush verdant green, moist with the morning's dew. There was no traffic on the roadway.

Nell steered her horse past Yoder's General Store, where she glimpsed the owner, Margaret Yoder, getting out of her buggy. Margaret made eye contact with her, and Nell lifted a hand in greeting. The woman smiled and waved back.

It wasn't long before she caught sight of Abram's farm ahead. She clicked on her directional signal and slowed Daisy to turn into the barnyard.

Nell saw Abram and Charlotte's eleven-year-old daughter, Rose Ann, as she came out of the house. Nell waved and climbed out of the open buggy and secured her horse.

"Nell!" Rose Ann cried. "Have you come to see Buddy?"

"*Ja*, Rosie. How is she doing?"

The child frowned. "I don't know. *Dat* won't let me near her."

"That's probably for the best. He doesn't want you to get hurt. Buddy's in pain and may kick out or nip you. You had best listen to your *vadder* and wait outside while I check on her."

Nate Peachy came out of the house. "*Gut* morning, Nell. Here to check on our mare?"

"*Ja*, Nate. I was telling your sister that it's best if she stays out here."

Nate smiled at his little sister. "Listen to her, Rose Ann. You know what *Dat* said."

"That I should stay out of the barn until *Dat*, you, Nell or James Pierce tells me I can visit Buddy."

"*Gut* girl," Nate praised. He led Nell into the barn. They eyed the mare silently for a moment before he turned to her. "You need anything?"

"*Nay*, if I do, I'll let you know." Nell smiled as the horse approached. "*Hallo*, Buddy," she greeted softly as the mare poked her head over the top of her stall.

"I'll leave you alone then," Nate murmured.

"*Danki*, Nate."

After Nate had left, Nell returned her attention to the horse.

"How are you feeling today, girl?" She reached toward the mare's head and stroked Buddy between the eyes then down her nose. "Are you in pain?"

She examined the area of the wound, where James had secured a bandage over the laceration. She was relieved to see that there was no blood seeping through the gauze. "Looks like you've not bled through. That's a *gut* thing."

Had James mentioned how long Abram should keep the bandage on? Nell frowned. Longer than one day, she was sure, but for how long? Had Abram given Buddy her medication?

"Did you eat breakfast, Buddy? Did you have your medicine?" She smiled when Buddy butted gently against her hand with her nose. "I'll have to speak with Abram," she told her. "We want you well and happy again." She spoke soothingly to the horse while she stroked her nose and the side of her neck.

She felt someone's presence in the barn before she heard a familiar voice.

"Nell."

"James!" She blinked and stared at him, taken aback by her stark awareness of him. This morning he wore a blue short-sleeved shirt with jeans and sneakers. She swallowed as emotion hit her square in the chest at the sight of him looking so tall, masculine and handsome. "I didn't expect to see you here."

"I see we shared the same thought." His warm smile made her heart race. "Buddy." His soft expression made her feel warm inside. "What made you come?"

"I was worried about her."

He approached, opened the stall and slipped inside. Buddy snorted and shifted uneasily. James set down his medical bag, then turned to the horse.

Nell watched as James spoke to the mare. She was amazed how well the animal responded to his deep, masculine tones.

He placed a calming hand on a spot not far from the wound as he bent low to examine the area around the bandage. "No infection to the surrounding tissue. She looks good." He glanced up at her when Nell remained silent. He searched her features as if he found something interesting in them.

Nell blushed, quickly agreed and glanced toward the horse.

"When does she need her dressing changed?" She kept her gaze on Buddy. The man's unexpected presence made her feel off-kilter.

"We probably should change it now since you're here and can assist. I'd like a closer look at her sutures." He opened the stall door to invite Nell inside. "Are you up for it?"

"Why wouldn't I be?" Nell asked, excited to learn something new.

The confines of the space seemed smaller than it had when she and James had come to take care of Buddy's injury the previous night.

As she stood by ready to assist, Nell was conscious of the man beside her as he worked. Fortunately, she was able to focus on the task and was ready with whatever he needed. Buddy shifted and snorted in protest as James carefully peeled back the bandage. Nell quickly stroked and spoke to sooth her until the mare settled down.

She watched as James checked the wound. He pressed gently on the surrounding area, and Buddy didn't seemed to mind. He stood back. "It looks great."

Nell silently agreed. She was amazed how well the sutures appeared. James had done an excellent job with them.

"Nell, would you please see if you can find the antiseptic ointment that's in my bag?"

She quickly found the tube and handed it to him along with a fresh dressing. He eyed her with approval as he took them from her.

"Thank you."

Nell nodded. She observed as James spread ointment on a clean square of gauze before he placed it carefully over Buddy's wound. She handed him the roll of surgical tape, and he secured the bandage in place.

James stood. "That should last until we see her next, unless a problem arises."

"I can stop by and check in a day or two," she offered.

He stared at her. "That would be helpful. Thank you."

They gazed at one another for several seconds. Nell felt a fluttering in her stomach. She looked away.

"Are you headed to the clinic next?" she asked as she left the stall with James following closely behind.

He glanced at his watch. "It's early, but I do have paperwork to catch up on." He smiled at her. "You're not due in for another hour."

"Is there something you need done?"

He hesitated. "Nothing that can't wait."

"I don't mind starting early," she said.

Something flickered in the depths of his dark eyes. "I don't want to take advantage, Nell."

"You won't be. If I can help before the clinic opens, I'll be happy to come." Nell headed toward her buggy.

James approached his car, which was parked several yards from her pony cart. "I'll see you there then."

She paused before climbing into her vehicle. "How is your leg?" she asked conversationally. She felt the intensity of his gaze and faced him. She'd seen him grimace when he'd stood after bending to examine Buddy and knew it had to be hurting him.

He didn't respond immediately. "Better today than yesterday."

"Gut." The realization that she had the ability to read him so well alarmed her.

"Nell—"

The ringing of his cell phone stopped his words. Nell waited patiently while James spoke to the person on the other end. When his face darkened, Nell became concerned.

"I'll be there as soon as I can," he said. He glanced at the thick-banded watch on his left wrist. "About ten, fifteen minutes." He listened silently. "Yes." He turned away from Nell, and she heard him issuing concise directions on what the caller should do until he arrived.

Suddenly feeling as if she was intruding on his phone conversation, she moved away to give him privacy.

James finished up his call and approached her with a look of apology. "Emergency," he said. "I guess I won't be doing paperwork this morning." He drew a sharp breath. "Want to come?" He explained about an injured dog that had been found on a man's back patio. "He's severely wounded."

"Ja," she agreed. "I'd like to help."

"It's not far."

Nell felt James's urgency as she left her pony cart and hurried toward his car. "Nate!" she called as she saw Abram's son coming around from the back of the barn. "We have to leave. Animal medical emergency. Is it *oll recht* if I leave my cart?"

"I'll drive it home for you," he offered.

She opened her mouth to object, but James said, "Thank you, Nate. I'll drive Nell home after work today."

Nell slid into the passenger side and buckled her seat belt as James climbed in beside her. He turned to face her in his seat.

"I should have asked you if it's all right if I drive you home," he said.

"'Tis fine," she assured him.

James gazed at her a long moment, nodded and then concentrated on putting the car into gear and driving off Abram's property.

James had visions of the injured canine as he drove toward Fred Moreland's farm. From Fred's description, the dog was covered with blood and in a terrible state. It was the reason he told Fred not to move the animal.

He was conscious of Nell beside him as he

drove. Would she be upset by the sight of the injured dog? He frowned. He hoped not. She'd been of tremendous help to him and hoped to keep her working at the clinic for the rest of the week.

Fred waited for him at the end of his front yard as James pulled into the man's driveway and parked close to the house. He got out of the car with his medical bag while Nell climbed out on the other side.

"Where is he?" James asked as Fred approached.

"In the back." The older man looked anxious.

He turned to Nell with concern. "Nell, this could be…"

"I'll be fine, James."

He set his medical kit not far from the little dog. He caught a glimpse of white fur beneath all the dirt and blood. He heard Nell's horrified gasp as she got her first look at the dog, but she didn't say anything as she quickly opened his medical kit and got to work.

"Is he yours?" James asked Fred.

"No. He's a stray. I don't have any barbed wire, but it looks like he got caught up in some. Not sure where."

The animal lay on its side on the concrete patio. He was breathing steadily, which was a good thing. James was prepared for the dog to snap and try to bite when he touched him. "Nell."

"I'm here," she said calmly. "I'll hold him

while you give him the injection." She busily prepared the syringe that he would need as he studied her. He could see tears shimmering in her pretty brown eyes.

Nell handed him the syringe and vial of local anesthetic, then she hunkered down by the animal's head and placed her hands on an uninjured area of the small body.

As she touched him, the dog's eyes opened and he looked as if he would struggle to rise, but Nell quickly soothed him with soft words and a gentle stroke. James regarded her a few seconds, amazed by her ability once again, before he found a small area appropriate for the shot. Nell's soft soothing voice continued, and James found that it calmed him as much as it did the injured dog.

"Nell, get me that brown bottle, too, please. I think it will be best to lightly sedate him. It will make things easier for him."

Nell obeyed, and James gave the dog another injection.

"We'll wait a few moments, and then we'll clean him up and take care of his wounds." James eyed the dog, deciding how best to proceed. "Would you please get us a bowl of warm water and an old towel?"

"Certainly," Fred agreed and hurried to do his bidding.

James and Nell were left alone on the man's

back patio with the injured animal. "Are you all right?" he asked.

"I'm fine." She hesitated as she studied the dog. "Do you think he got tangled in barbed wire or did someone abuse him?"

James regarded the animal with a frown. "I suspect he was abused."

"Fred?"

"No," he said. "Absolutely not. Fred is one of my clients. He's got a soft touch for all animals. I take care of his cat and dog. It's easy to tell that he loves them. His wife died recently, and his animals give him comfort."

James turned his focus back to the dog and wondered whether or not he should move him. Would it be better to treat him inside?

Before James could decide, Fred returned with an old but clean white enamel basin filled with warm water. He set it, a soft washcloth and towel within James's reach. He had draped a folded blanket over his arm.

"I thought you might want to move him onto this. It's soft and may be more comfortable for him." He dropped down on one knee and unfolded the quilt. "It's okay if it gets wet or dirty. I don't like seeing this little guy on the concrete."

"You found him here?" Nell asked softly.

"Yes. I came out this morning to have my coffee as I often do, when I saw him. That's when I called you, Dr. Pierce. I was afraid to touch or to move him. I didn't want to hurt him, and I didn't know if he'd bite if I tried."

"It was good that you let him be and called me, Fred." James eyed the unfolded blanket in Fred's arms. "You grab an end and we'll spread it out."

With Nell and James's help, Fred folded the quilt into quarters, then spread it over the concrete patio. James and Fred carefully eased the animal from the concrete onto the padded folds.

Nell grabbed the washcloth and dipped it into the warm water. She placed the towel within easy reach and began to clean the area about the animal's neck.

James went to work cleaning the actual wounds with antiseptic cleansing pads. He cleaned a wound on the side of the dog's belly. It looked as if he'd been burned as well as cut.

Nell met his gaze. "He *was* abused."

He nodded as he felt the anger inside him grow.

Fred had gone into the house for more linens. He came out in time to hear Nell's comment. "Someone did this to him?" He looked pale and upset.

"Yes, I'm afraid so." James didn't look up from his task.

"Whoever did this should be in jail," the older man said.

"If he's ever caught, he will be."

"Have you seen much of this before?" Nell asked, her voice sounding shaky.

"Too many times." He carefully washed each wound while Nell cleaned the surrounding areas. "Did you see him walk?" he asked Fred.

"No. He was lying here. I supposed he was able to move well enough to get here."

James went on to check the animal's legs and was upset to find one that appeared to be broken.

"Fred, while he's knocked out, I'm going to take him back to my office. I want to do X-rays. One leg is broken, but until I see the extent of the damage, I won't know the best way to treat him."

"What are you going to do with him then?" Fred eyed the animal with longing. "Do you think I'll be able to keep him?"

"If the leg is bad, I may have to amputate."

He heard Nell's sharp inhalation of breath.

"Doesn't matter to me. Dogs can get by with three legs. I still want him."

"What about Max?" James asked of the man's other dog.

"This one will be fine with him. Max will like the company. I'll keep them apart until this little guy is well enough."

"If you're going to keep him, maybe you should come up with a name for him."

Fred thought for a moment.

"How about Joseph?" Nell suggested. "You can

call him Joey." When Fred looked at her, she explained, "Joseph means 'addition,' and this little guy will be a new addition to your family."

Fred smiled. "I like it. Joey it is. Max and Joey."

Nell nodded, then returned her attention to patting dry the area she'd washed.

"We should move him while he's still sedated," James said. "I've got a small stretcher in the trunk of my car."

"I'll get it," Fred offered, and James handed him the keys.

The man was back in less than a minute. He set the stretcher on the ground, then the three of them took hold of the edges of the blanket and set Joey on the stretcher. James and Fred lifted the stretcher and carried it to the car, setting it carefully on the backseat. Without being told, Nell climbed into the back with Joey.

"I'll give you a call to let you know how he makes out," James said.

"I want him, James," Fred repeated. "No matter what."

James climbed into the front seat and glanced back to see Nell buckled into her seat belt and leaning over Joey while stroking his head tenderly. "Nell." She looked at him. "He'll make it."

"I hope so." She blinked rapidly as if fighting back tears.

James felt the strongest desire to take Nell into his arms to comfort her. But he ignored it and instead drove back toward the clinic.

He'd been thinking of Nell too much lately. He wasn't sure what to do, but he knew he couldn't risk hurting the young Amish woman who'd worked her way into his affections.

He reminded himself that he just had to make it through the end of the week. Once Michelle and Janie were back in the office, Nell would return to her Amish life and he'd be able to put her out of his mind.

At least, he hoped so.

Chapter Six

Nell felt her throat tighten and her eyes fill with tears as she gently stroked the injured puppy. Who could do such a thing to one of God's poor defenseless creatures?

She looked into the rearview mirror and asked James, "Do you think he'll make it?"

"He will if I can have anything to do with it."

She knew what he meant. James would do all he could, but ultimately the dog's recovery would be in God's hands.

Soon James was pulling into the clinic parking lot. He parked near the door, then got out to help with Joey.

Nell opened her door. "How are we going to do this?"

James eyed the little dog. "I'll carry him." He bent inside and, using the sides of the blanket, he scooped him up carefully. "Nell, would you get my keys? They're on the front seat."

One look at James's expression had her melting inside. The man was obviously as upset about Joey as she was. Enough that he'd forgotten to grab his keys.

James had straightened with the dog in his arms. "Would you open the door? It's the blue key."

She found the right one and hurried to open the building. She turned on the light and then held the door open for James.

James quickly went to the treatment area. He gently set Joey down on an examination table. "We have to x-ray him. I'm afraid he may have several broken bones—not just a broken leg."

Nell sent up a silent prayer, then whispered, "I hope not."

James checked the dog's heart and breathing with his stethoscope before he moved him over to the platform under the X-ray machine.

"Will he sleep for a while?" Nell asked with concern. She hated the thought that Joey might wake and be in pain. He might get scared and struggle, further injuring himself.

"Yes, long enough. He'll be groggy when he does finally come out of it."

Nell stood by ready to help as James prepared the machine. She helped shift the dog into different positions and then waited while James snapped the photos. Little Joey remained sedated while they worked.

Nell felt her nerves stretch taut as she waited for the results of the X-rays.

"He has a break in his hind leg," James said after reading the films for several long moments.

"Will he be all right?"

"I can't promise, but there is a good chance his leg will heal. We'll have to splint it. Unlike Jonas's injury, this little guy will have his leg bound for several weeks."

He stepped away from the X-ray light panel and moved toward Joey. "There doesn't appear to be any new bleeding, but I'm going to suture the worst of his wounds."

Nell kept her eyes on the little dog. She was feeling emotional. The news that the animal's leg wouldn't need to be amputated had buoyed her spirits, but she still had a hard time accepting that someone could be so cruel to the little dog.

She knew others within her Amish community didn't understand her love for animals. They took good care of their horses, which they needed, and their other farm animals, but they didn't feel the same about dogs or cats. No one within her church community would intentionally hurt an animal, she didn't think. And they'd come to accept that her concern for animals made her a good person to call on when they needed help with them.

Working with James was teaching her how to better help her neighbors and friends…and gave her a sense of purpose.

She settled her gaze on James. His attention was on Joey, his eyes focused on the dog's little body as he meticulously stitched closed one wound before moving to another.

She concentrated on the work so that she could ignore her growing feelings for the man. She gasped, struck anew by how much she liked spending time with James.

James looked up at her, a frown settling on his brow. "Are you all right?"

She managed a smile. "*Ja*, I'm fine." She hesitated as he returned his attention to Joey. "How is he?"

"I think he'll make it, but seeing what was done to him—" She could feel his anger and understood it despite God's teachings.

"Will he have to spend the night?" she asked.

"I think it would be a good idea."

"I can stay," she offered.

He glanced at her then, his expression soft. "I appreciate it, Nell, but I'll stay. Your family will be worried about you, and I know what to do if something goes wrong."

She felt a sharp tightening in her chest. "Do you expect something to go wrong?"

"I don't know, but better to be safe than sorry." He grabbed a spoon splint and cut it to the correct size before he began to tape it onto Joey's broken leg. He paused to reach into his jeans pocket and pulled out a sheet of paper. "Would you call Fred and let him know?"

"*Ja*, of course." She took the phone number and abruptly left the room. After she told Fred how Joey was doing, she took a minute to compose herself before heading to the treatment area again.

James didn't look up as he continued to stabilize Joey's broken leg. "Did you reach Fred?" he asked.

"*Ja*. He was upset but eager for Joey to get well."

James straightened and turned to face her. A small smile hovered on his lips. "Fred's a good man. Joey will have a good home."

Nell's throat was tight, and she didn't want to break down in front of him. She didn't want for him to believe that she couldn't handle the work. The last thing she wanted was to lose this position.

"Now what?" she asked.

"We'll make him comfortable, and I'll see how he is when he wakes up. I'll move him into a kennel right now. We'll be able to keep an eye on him while we see patients."

She waited while he gently moved Joey and then headed back out to the front desk area where she pulled out the appointment book and prepared for the day.

It was seven forty-five when she unlocked the door. James's first patient with its owner was already waiting to come in.

The day went quickly because of their full patient schedule and their vigil of Joey. Soon, it was time for Nell to go home. James said that he would take her home, but she felt bad for making him leave Joey for even a few moments.

"I can call someone to drive me," she offered.

James shook his head. "No it's fine. I can take you home."

She waited while he checked on Joey one more time, and then they headed outside. He unlocked his car, then opened her door and waited until she was seated. His kindness made her feel both uncomfortable and somehow cherished.

The interior of the car seemed close, and she was overly conscious of the man beside her as he turned on the ignition, then backed away from the building.

She blinked back tears. What was she going to do? It was wrong to work with James when she had feelings for him. Yet, she couldn't leave the position. It would be unfair to force him to work alone in the practice, especially since she'd promised to help him. And he wasn't the one with the problem. She was.

Nell drew a steadying breath. It would be fine. She wouldn't let on how she felt. She'd finish the job and then get on with her life, taking with her new knowledge of animal care—and a longing for a life with someone she could never have.

James felt Nell's presence keenly as he exited the parking lot. "Which way?"

"Left."

As he drove, he remembered her making a left when she'd departed yesterday.

She was silent as he headed down the road. He flashed her a quick look, wondering how she was feeling. She glanced toward the window but not before he saw her tears.

"Nell." Instinctively, he reached out and captured her hand where it rested on the seat beside her. He felt her stiffen and then look at him with brimming eyes. "He'll be all right."

She blinked rapidly, and he quickly released her hand.

"I'm sorry," she said.

He flashed her a startled glance. "What for?"

"I'm not a *gut* assistant if I cry about a patient, am I?"

"Nell, your compassion, your empathy makes you a great assistant."

"Then you're not disappointed in me?"

"For what?" he said. "For caring?" He paused. "Of course not." He drove past Whittier's Store and Lapp's Carriage Shop.

"Take the next left to get to our farm."

James made the turn and saw a farmhouse up ahead. "Here?" he asked.

"Ja."

Minutes later, he pulled into the barnyard. As he pulled the car to a stop, four young women exited the house. "Your sisters?"

She nodded as she opened the door and climbed out.

"How's the little dog?" a young redhead asked. "Will he be *oll recht*?"

"We don't know for certain, but we think so."

A dark-haired young woman bent to look inside the car.

"Hello," he said.

"You must be James," she said.

He inclined his head. "I am."

Nell quickly introduced him to her sisters.

"We did what we could for him. I'll know tomorrow morning." He glanced at Nell. "I need to head back."

"Let me know how he does?"

"I will." He gazed at her, interested to see

her surrounded by her sisters. "I'll see you in the morning."

"*Ja*, I'll see you then."

James put the vehicle into Reverse and then turned toward the road. He saw that Nell's father and mother had joined her sisters in the yard. He waved at them as he drove off. He would have liked to stay, but he needed to get back to Joey. The last thing he wanted was for the dog to wake up and start to chew on his wounds.

Before he pulled onto the road, he took one last look toward the Stoltzfus residence. Seeing Nell with her family made him feel things he hadn't felt in a long time.

"How was your day at the clinic?" Arlin Stoltzfus asked Nell.

"I'd say *gut*, but we're treating an abused and severely injured dog. Seeing Joey suffer was anything but *gut*, *Dat*."

"Was that why Dr. Pierce left in a hurry?"

"*Ja*. Joey should wake up soon. James needs to be near when he does."

"He's *gut* at what he does," her father said.

"*Ja*, *Dat*," Nell said. "He is."

"You have two days left in his employ."

Nell felt a sudden uncomfortable feeling inside. "*Ja*. Tomorrow and Friday—and I'll be done."

She sensed someone's curious gaze and turned to see her sister Leah studying her closely.

"He seems like a *gut* man," Ellie said.

"He is," Nell admitted.

"An *Englisher*," *Dat* said as if he had to remind her.

"*Ja*, he is," Nell said, meeting her father's gaze directly. Arlin nodded as if satisfied by what he saw in her expression. "You know his family. You've spoken with him. He is an honorable man."

She thought it wise to change the topic of conversation. "How is Jonas? Did he behave today?"

"He always behaves." Charlie's features softened with affection. It seemed that her sister loved the dog almost as much as she. Nell knew she could trust her youngest sister to take good care of him.

"'Tis hard to believe he'd injured his leg," Leah commented.

"I'm thankful that he fully recovered."

The family headed toward the house. "Anyone hungry?" *Mam* asked.

Nell looked at her gratefully. "I am."

"We all are." Ellie glanced back. "Meg? Why are you lagging behind?"

"I'm coming."

Nell waited for Meg to catch up. "Anything wrong?"

Meg shook her head.

"Are you sure?"

Her sister smiled. "*Ja. Danki*, Nell."

"I'll be happy to listen if you need to talk."

"I'll keep that in mind." Meg ran ahead to join Ellie and Charlie who had climbed the front porch after their parents.

She and Leah followed more slowly as the others entered the house.

"Two days more and then you're done working for James," Leah said. She paused. "How do you feel about it?"

Nell shrugged. "Fine. I've learned a lot this week, but I have things here that need to be done."

Leah narrowed her gaze. "Like what?"

"Like care for my animals. 'Tis not fair that my sisters have to do the work."

"We don't mind. Charlie loves taking care of them, especially Jonas." Her sister reached for the handle and pulled open the door. "But I agree that you have something that needs to be done." When Nell met her gaze, she said, "You need to find yourself a husband before *Dat* gets impatient and finds one for you."

Nell experienced an overwhelming sorrow. If Michael hadn't died, they would have been married, and she would have had children by now. She kept her thoughts to herself. None of them knew about Michael and that was a good thing. She had the choice back when she'd met Michael.

As a full member of the church, she no longer had the option of falling for an *Englisher*.

She still felt a tightening in her chest for her loss and what might have been had Michael lived.

Chapter Seven

After she'd enjoyed a delicious meal of fried chicken, vegetables and warm bread slathered with butter, Nell stood on the front porch and stared out into the yard. Her thoughts went to little Joey—and James. She had the strongest urge to ride over to the clinic and see how the dog was faring. But she couldn't. Thoughts of Michael made her particularly lonely this evening. It wouldn't be wise to see James, the only man she'd been attracted to since Michael's death.

She climbed down from the porch and crossed the yard to the barn, drawn once again to her animals for solace. James's attempt to comfort her earlier when she'd begun to cry had startled her. The warmth of his fingers covering hers had made feel things she had no right to feel about the *Englisher*.

She had just been upset over Joey, she reasoned. But was that it? She sighed. *Nay*, she'd felt an attraction to him well before they'd treated Joey.

Entering the barn, Nell went to the horses first. She rubbed Daisy between the eyes, then moved to pay similar attention to their other mare, Lily. She ensured each horse had enough water inside the barn and filled the trough in the pasture.

"Do you want to go outside?" she asked the horses when she went back inside. "'Tis a beautiful evening. You can enjoy it for a little while."

Daisy's stall was next to Lily's. She took her out of her stall and released her into the fenced area before she did the same for Lily. Nell felt her lips curve as the two mares galloped into the field. They chased each other in play before they settled down to leisurely munch on pasture grass.

Satisfied that the mares would be fine for a while, Nell stopped back in the barn to visit Ed, their gelding, and her dog, Jonas. Excited to see her, her little dog whimpered and jumped up on his hind legs. When he put his front paws on her skirt, Nell grinned, certain more than ever his leg was completely healed from the injuries he'd received when she witnessed some teenagers throw him out of their moving car.

"Let's not overdo it, Jonas." She gently repositioned Jonas's front paws onto the ground, then knelt next to him. The dog instantly rolled onto his back, exposing his belly. Nell laughed as she wove her fingers through his fur and rubbed.

"Nell?"

"In here!" she called.

Leah stepped into the light. "I thought I'd find you here." She opened the stall door and slipped in to join her. After closing the door carefully behind her, she squatted beside Nell. "Are you *oll recht*?"

"*Ja*, why wouldn't I be?"

Leah's expression turned somber. "What happened earlier?"

"What do you mean?"

"You were upset when James brought you home."

"Joey," Nell said. "What happened to him was heartbreaking."

"I'm sorry," Leah said softly.

Nell felt a clenching in her belly. "Me, too," she said. She continued to stroke Jonas, who clearly loved every moment of her attention. She bit her lip. "*Dat* seemed angry when James brought me home."

"I don't think he was angry. I think he was concerned."

"Why?"

"Because he's an *Englisher,* and he's handsome."

"*Ja*, he is," Nell murmured in agreement.

Leah stared. "Nell, are you falling for him?"

"Nay," Nell said quickly. Too quickly. She had to admit that there was something about him that drew her like a moth to a flame. But she wouldn't give in.

They walked toward the fence to watch the horses. "Are you sure?" Leah asked.

Nell inclined her head.

Her sister sighed. *"Gut."*

Ellie suddenly joined her sisters at the fence rail. "'Twas a delicious supper, *ja, schweschter*?"

Nell and Leah exchanged amused glances. *"Ja,* it was," Nell agreed.

"Will you bring the dog—Joey—home once he's well?"

Nell shook her head. *"Nay,* the man who found Joey wants him. He lives alone and dotes on his pets. Joey will have a *gut* home with him." She offered a silent prayer that Joey's condition didn't worsen.

"Come inside," Ellie urged. *"Mam* brought out dessert, and she and *Dat* are waiting for you."

"I'm not particularly hungry." But Nell knew her parents would be upset if she didn't return to the table.

"She made carrot cake," Ellie told her. "Your favorite."

"Sounds *gut* to me." Leah grinned.

"I guess I could eat a piece."

"Race you!" Ellie challenged.

The three sisters hurried across the lawn, up the porch and into the house.

James checked on Joey in his kennel several times during the evening. When he saw the little dog was resting comfortably, he relaxed and went to his office to do paperwork. He'd finished what he needed to for the day when he heard the dog whimper.

He hurried toward the treatment area. Mindful of the extent of Joey's injuries, James opened the kennel door and pulled him gently into his arms.

"Who did this to you, little one?" he whispered. He stroked the little dog's head as he moved toward a treatment table. If he ever discovered who it was, he'd call the authorities and have them prosecuted for animal cruelty.

He found some pain medicine and administered it to Joey. "This will make you feel better for a while, little one. I'll stay the night, and if you're better tomorrow, we'll call Fred and he can come for you."

He picked Joey up and held the dog close to his chest. Joey must have sensed that James wouldn't hurt him as the animal burrowed his head closer. James narrowed his gaze as he examined a small wound along the side of his neck. He didn't like the look of it. He grabbed a canister of antiseptic from a cabinet and sprayed it on the wound.

"Don't worry, Joey," he soothed when Joey struggled. "I won't hurt you. I'm here to help." What he wouldn't give to have Nell by his side assisting him. But it was late, and she'd already put in longer than a full day's work.

After setting Joey back in his kennel, James went to the refrigerator in the clinic's kitchenette, searching for some leftover pizza. When he was done eating, he went back to his office to make a few phone calls to check up on his patients. Afterward, he went into a storage closet and pulled out the cot he kept here in case he might need to sleep at the clinic.

He made up the cot, and then wondered what he'd do to fill the remaining hours until bed. He found the paperback book he'd started one afternoon before he'd moved back to Lancaster County and became engrossed in the story. He stopped once to give Joey another dosage of pain medication, then went back to the book.

The next thing he knew, he'd read through half of it, and it was late enough to sleep. He checked on Joey one last time. Satisfied the dog would sleep the night, James lay on his cot and closed his eyes.

Nell arrived for work at seven forty-five the next morning. James had been leaving the back entrance unlocked for her. There was no sign of him in the treatment room when she walked in. She peeked into an exam room but didn't see him. *"Hallo?"*

"I'm up front, Nell!" she heard him call out.

She made her way toward the reception area. As she entered the room, she caught sight of James bent over Michelle's desk, his eyes focused on the computer screen. As if sensing her presence, he looked up.

"Hi." He straightened. "Is it eight already?"

"It's a quarter to." She approached and placed her purse under the desk where she sometimes stashed it. "What are you doing?"

"Updating health records on the computer," he said. "Not my favorite thing to do. Michelle usually does it for me. I did some of them last night but—" He keyed in another entry then stood, looking pleased. "There. I'm all finished. Michelle will be proud."

Nell felt a rush of pleasure upon seeing his grin. Mention of the previous night brought her thoughts back to their patient. "How's Joey doing?"

"He's doing well. In fact, I think I'll give Fred a call later today. I think it will be good for Joey to recover in his new home."

"I'm glad he's doing better."

"Me, too." James frowned. "I wish I knew

who did this to him. Whoever it was should be held accountable."

"By whom?"

"Animal cruelty is against the law." He moved out from behind the desk, and Nell took his place.

She opened the appointment book to check on the number of scheduled patients. "There are only three appointments in the book today, and two are reschedules from Friday."

"Only three?" He sounded disappointed.

"We may have another emergency," she said. "Not that we want one," she added quickly, blushing. She knew he was working hard to grow his practice and realized that a schedule like today's wasn't encouraging. "Your first patient doesn't come in until ten."

"We'll check on Joey, then call Fred afterward."

The morning appointments went smoothly. Mrs. Rogan arrived with Boots, and a kitten in a cat carrier. Nell didn't have any experience with cats. She liked them, but they didn't have any on the farm. While they waited for James to finish up with Boots, Nell cradled the kitten in her arms, enjoying the way it purred and cuddled against her.

"She likes you," Mrs. Rogan said with a smile.

"She's sweet."

"Would you like to have one?" the woman asked. "Mimi came from my neighbor's cat's litter. She has three sisters and two brothers. They all need good homes."

Nell thought of how accepting her father had been of all her animals. But she worried if Jonas and a kitten would get along. If not, would *Dat* allow him in the house? She doubted it. She sighed. She really wanted a kitten. "Do Boots and Mimi get along?"

"Oh, my, yes, dear. Mimi even snuggles up to Boots to nap. He seems to enjoy her company."

"I'd like to have one, but I have a dog."

"I'm sure Jonas and a kitten will get along fine," James said. "When a cat is a kitten, it's a great time to introduce the two. Boots here likes Mimi, don't you, boy?" He smiled and rubbed the dog's neck.

"But Jonas lives in the barn," she said. "He does have his own stall. I fixed it up for him."

"I don't doubt that," James said, lending his support. "Nell is a wonderful assistant," he told Mrs. Rogan.

Nell blushed as the woman studied her. "I'm sure she is." She studied her kitten in Nell's arms. "I can bring you a kitten if you'd like. Any particular color?"

"The color doesn't matter."

"I'll pick one out for you then." She beamed at Nell. "Betty—my neighbor—will be so pleased that I've found a home for another kitten."

She checked the woman out at the front desk. "May I help you to your car?"

Mrs. Rogan looked pleased. "Thank you, Nell. You're very kind."

Nell took the kitten's carrier while Mrs. Rogan held on to her purse and Boots's leash. When the woman and her animals were settled in the car, Nell said, "Mrs. Rogan? Would you like to take a few of Dr. Pierce's business cards with you? He hasn't been in our area long. I'm sure he'd appreciate any referrals."

"What an excellent idea, Nell. I'll be happy to pass them to all my animal-loving friends. I've been extremely pleased with Dr. Pierce's care."

Nell hurried inside, grabbed a stack of cards and quickly returned. She handed them to Mrs. Rogan. "Thank you again."

"My pleasure."

Nell felt a sense of accomplishment as the woman drove away. Why hadn't she thought of this sooner? When she'd brought Jonas in originally to be treated for his injuries, James hadn't charged her. He'd asked if she'd spread the word about his practice instead. And she had, but not as much as she could have. James's concern over the number of patients made her realize that she could do more to help grow his practice.

He looked up with a heart-stopping smile. "Mrs. Rogan gone?"

Nell nodded. She hesitated and then asked, "Do you think I'm foolish for wanting a kitten?"

James blinked. "No. Why would you think that? The kitten will have a wonderful home with you"

She felt a rush of warmth. "I'll do my best," she said.

Surprisingly the phone rang moments after Mrs. Rogan left, and James answered it. "We have another appointment for tomorrow afternoon—Betty Desmond, a friend of Mrs. Rogan. Mrs. Rogan must have called her on her cell as she was leaving."

Nell hid a smile. "Did she say who she's bringing in?"

"A litter of kittens. You'll be able to pick out the one you want."

"I'd take all of them if I could. As it is, I'll have some convincing to do at home." But she wasn't worried. Her father was lenient when it came to her and her animals.

Nell turned away. "I'll set things up for tomorrow."

"Thank you, Nell."

She cleaned the exam rooms in preparation

for the next day—her last one. There were now seven patients scheduled for tomorrow. Wearing protective gloves, Nell washed instruments, then placed them into the autoclave. She turned on the machine as James had taught her, then went to refill the disposables in the treatment room. One accidentally slipped out from her hand. She reached to retrieve it just as James bent to get it for her. They bumped foreheads as he rose with item in hand.

"Are you all right?" he asked with concern.

Nell felt her heart start to pound at his nearness. They were eye to eye, close enough that she glimpsed tiny golden flecks in his dark eyes.

She swallowed against a suddenly dry throat. "I'm fine," she said, aware of the huskiness in her voice.

James stared at her, a strange look settling on his features. "Nell."

Nell couldn't seem to tear her gaze away. She felt her chest tighten and an odd little tingle run from her nape down the length of her spine.

James's only thought was of how lovely Nell was both inside and out. He couldn't remember the last time he had feelings for a woman. And this one was more than special.

Suddenly he leaned forward and gently placed his lips against hers.

He heard her gasp, but she didn't pull away. His head lifted, and he searched her eyes. She looked thunderstruck and adorable. He bent again and took one last sweet kiss before he pulled abruptly away. "I'm sorry."

She gazed at him, apparently speechless.

"Nell—"

"I have to leave!" she gasped. "I'm sorry, but I won't be in tomorrow."

"Tomorrow is your last day, Nell," he reminded her. James felt a crushing sensation in his chest. "I promise it won't happen again—"

"*Nay*, I can't take the chance."

He studied her flushed cheeks, realized that she was not unaffected by his kiss.

"The office is ready for tomorrow. You should be fine without me. 'Tis only one day." She turned away and headed toward the front room.

"Nell." He saw her shoulders tense as she faced him. "I'm sorry if I've upset you, but I can't truly say that I regret kissing you."

She blanched, spun, then left in a hurry. He heard the front door open and shut. She had gone. Without saying goodbye.

James closed his eyes. What had he done? He should have known better. She was Amish; he was considered *English*. Their worlds were too different for them to be anything but friends.

He drew a sharp breath as the regret he'd claimed he hadn't felt suddenly filled him. His regret in chasing Nell away.

Chapter Eight

Nell was rattled as she drove home. James's kiss had taken her totally by surprise. She should have pushed him away, and the fact that she hadn't done so scared her. What shocked her the most was that she'd liked his kisses.

It was midafternoon when she steered her buggy into the yard. She knew her family would wonder why she wouldn't be returning to the clinic. It would be easy enough to explain why she was home early this afternoon, for there were no patients scheduled. It made sense to call the day to a close.

But James had seven patients to see tomorrow, and while she felt bad that he would have to manage on his own, she wasn't about to go back. She had to avoid James. Her feelings for him were too powerful. And now that she knew he was attracted to her, too…

To her relief, her family didn't pry into her reasons for not going back to work. Her father seemed pleased that she'd be at home, and for that she was relieved and grateful.

As she washed the dinner dishes alongside her sister Charlie, she wondered if James had called Fred about Joey. Then she mentally scolded herself. He probably had. Besides, Joey was no longer her concern.

That night as she went to bed, Nell couldn't help but recall the day's events. She sighed. There would be no returning to pick out a kitten. She could only imagine what Mrs. Rogan would think after she learned that Nell no longer worked there.

Moonlight filtered in through the sheer white curtains as Nell lay in bed and stared up at the ceiling. She couldn't stop thinking about James's kiss, his clean male scent with a hint of something. Cologne?

She was lonely. Was that why she'd reacted to James the way she had?

She became overwhelmed with sadness as she thought of Michael and the life she would have shared with him if he hadn't died. If she'd married Michael, she wouldn't be having these feelings about James.

She and Michael probably wouldn't have stayed in Happiness. They might not have moved far, but they would have lived perhaps within Lancaster

City, in a small home surrounded by neighboring houses. They would have had children and been happy together…if only Michael hadn't died.

Grief struck her hard, and her eyes filled with tears. *Oh, Michael…*

Lonely and heartbroken, Nell sobbed softly. Unable to control her sorrow, she climbed out of bed and went to look out the window. It was on a night like this that she had left the house to tell Michael that she'd decided to accept his marriage proposal. The moon had been large in the dark sky, the summer air had been warm and balmy, a perfect night for meeting the man she'd loved.

Only Michael hadn't come.

She'd waited for him for over two hours until finally, disappointed, she'd returned home. She'd reached the house and gone upstairs to bed. Then within an hour, her family had been on their way to the hospital after an ambulance had been called for Meg. Her sister had suffered excruciating abdominal pains.

Meg had been admitted to the hospital and spent several days in intensive care. A ruptured appendix had threatened her life.

Overcome with worry for her sister, Nell had attempted to put aside thoughts of Michael. But in those moments when she left Meg's hospital room to go to the cafeteria with her other sisters, Nell had suffered from more than concern.

What if Michael had come to their special spot the next night? What if he'd tried the following nights only to be disappointed when she didn't show?

During the afternoon of Meg's second day in the hospital, Nell had gone downstairs to buy a cup of tea, which she planned to take back to the room. Ellie, Leah and Charlie had gone home with *Mam* and *Dat* to pack a few items for Meg, to see to the animals and to get some sleep.

Mam and *Dat* had appeared to have aged since Meg was first brought in. The doctor had suggested that the family go home to eat properly and get some rest. Meg would need them at their best during her recovery. Nell had volunteered to stay until their return later that evening when she would head home for the night.

Nell had been returning with her tea when she'd heard loud sounds coming from inside a hospital room on Meg's floor. Without thought, she'd glanced inside and saw a man lying in the hospital bed, hooked up to oxygen and a heart monitor.

She could still recall with startling clarity the awful moment when she'd recognized the patient. The horrible sounds that had come from the heart monitor and oxygen pump had turned her blood to ice.

Michael. It had been her beloved Michael. Her

first instinct had been to go to him, but a nurse had stopped her.

"The patient isn't allowed visitors," she'd said.

Nell had wanted to cry out that she wasn't simply a visitor; she was the woman to whom he'd proposed marriage. The agony of seeing him in that bed, knowing that he was fighting for his life, was still painful to recall even after five years.

Her family didn't know about Michael. She and Michael had been meeting secretly as Amish sweethearts often did within her community. Only Michael wasn't Amish. He was an *Englisher*, but at the time, Nell could have left her community without reprisal. She hadn't joined the church yet, so she would have been free to leave.

The next day, after a night at home spent fervently praying, Nell returned to the hospital. She found Michael's bed empty as she passed by his room. Heart pounding hard, she'd asked at the nurses' station what happened to him.

She'd nearly fainted when she'd heard that Michael had died during the night.

In shock, Nell had gotten through each day focusing on her sister. She'd had no time to grieve or accept the fact that Michael was really gone. Afterward, she'd overheard the nurses talking. She learned that Michael's injuries had been sustained in a car accident when his vehicle was struck by a drunk driver's on the night they were to meet. She stared out into the moonlit yard and recalled the way she and Michael had met in a local grocery store. How they'd met up again in the same place on another day. Michael had been handsome and funny, and she'd fallen in love immediately.

After Meg recovered, Nell had decided to join the church. Couples usually joined prior to marrying, but Michael was the only man she'd ever love. There was no reason not to join the Amish church. She had lost Michael but she'd been grateful to the Lord for sparing Meg's life.

Nell turned from the window and went back to bed. And cried until she was so exhausted, she fell asleep.

The next morning, Nell climbed out of bed. She felt groggy from lack of sleep, but she knew she had work to do. She needed to feed and water the animals.

She smiled as she thought of her little dog. Nell was fortunate that her father tolerated her love of animals. After nearly losing her sister Meg, Arlin Stoltzfus had become lenient with all of his daughters.

She slipped out of the house and headed toward the barn. She took care of her pets and the farm animals, then returned to do her house chores.

There was laundry to do, dusting to be done, and floors to be swept.

She entered through the kitchen and grabbed the broom from the back room, continuing her day with housework instead of enjoying her last day at the clinic as planned. Her sisters joined in to help, and their happy chatter and teasing helped Nell get through the day.

That afternoon, Nell heard the sound of a buggy as she swept the front porch. She paused to watch as it parked near the house. Matthew Troyer got out of the vehicle.

He waved. "Nell!"

"*Hallo*, Matthew." She smiled, for the young man always appeared to be in good humor.

"I've brought you something." He skirted the vehicle, then bent into the passenger side to pick up a cardboard box.

Curious, Nell set aside her broom and descended the porch steps. "What is it?"

"Come and see."

She approached and peered into the box. "A kitten!" It was a tiny orange tabby. "Where did you—" she began. She blinked back tears as she met his gaze. "James."

"*Ja*, he asked me to bring her to you. Said you were interested in owning a kitten. He thought you might like this one best."

Emotion clogged Nell's throat as she reached

in to pick up the cat. "She's beautiful." Cuddling the kitten against her, she glanced at Matthew. "*Danki*, she's...perfect."

He eyed her with fond amusement. "James thought you'd say that."

Warmth infused her belly as she realized how well James knew her. "Please thank him for me."

"You can thank him yourself when you see him."

But would she ever see him again? Only if he came to a community gathering, which was entirely possible since his family belonged to her church.

Nell glanced back at the house for any sign of her father. She had to break the news to him that she now owned a kitten. "I need to make a place for him in the barn. He can share Jonas's stall."

Matthew blinked. "Wait! There's more." He reached into the back of the buggy for a bag of kitten food, a small scratching post and a small bed. "My *bruder* sent these, as well."

"He didn't have to do that," she said, but it didn't surprise her that he had. James was an extremely considerate man.

"This is James. You've worked with him. This is his way."

"*Ja*, I know."

"Let me carry these into the barn for you."

Nell stroked the tiny cat's head. "*Danki*, Matthew." She was aware of the young man following her as she entered the barn and headed toward her dog's stall. Jonas whimpered and ran toward her as she pulled the door and held it open for Matthew. "You have a new friend, Jonas," she said. "You'll be nice to her, *ja*?"

She hunkered down to allow Jonas to sniff the kitten. She waited with bated breath to see how he would react to his new roommate. Nell grew concerned when Jonas growled and backed away. "Jonas! She won't hurt you. She's just a little thing. Come and meet her."

"He's growling at me, not her," Matthew said as he set the bed near Jonas's and the post in the opposite corner of the stall. "Where do you want her food?"

"You can put it there for now." She gestured toward a table in the back of the stall. "I'll move it later."

Jonas continued to growl, and Nell saw that Matthew was right. The dog was nervous of Matt, not the kitten.

Matthew crouched next to her and held out his hand. "Come. I'll not hurt you. I'm Nell's friend."

Nell flashed him a look, but Matthew was too busy trying to gain her dog's trust to notice her.

"Jonas! Come." The animal gazed at her with trepidation. "'Tis Matthew. He's James's *bruder*. You know James. He took *gut* care of you when you were hurt." She felt a pang in her heart as she mentioned his name.

Matthew didn't move. He waited patiently until finally Jonas inched closer. Although he and James were stepsiblings, they both shared the same patient and compassionate nature. Nell experienced a wave of affection toward Matthew.

The young man didn't speak. He simply stayed in his crouched position with his hand extended toward Jonas.

Finally, Jonas came close enough to sniff his hand then started to lick his fingers. Matthew laughed. "He's a *gut* one, isn't he?" he said with a smile.

"*Ja*, he is. And you were right—he was afraid of you, not this little one."

He regarded her with amusement. "Are you going to keep calling her *little one*, or will you be naming her?"

She made a face at him. "Any suggestions?"

"*Kotz?*"

"I'm not going to call her cat!"

He laughed, and the sound was delightful. "You asked for a suggestion," he reminded her.

"Not a bad one."

Matthew placed his hand over his heart. "You wound me, and I was trying to be helpful."

"Poor Matthew."

He grinned at her. "Nell?"

She set the kitten within distance of Jonas, who

didn't seem to be alarmed or angry at its presence. "I think they'll get along."

"Nell." His tone had changed, become serious.

Frowning, she met his gaze. "Is something wrong?"

He shook his head. "I was wondering if you'd be attending the youth singing on Sunday."

"I haven't been to a singing in years."

"Would you consider it?" He paused. "I'd like to take you home afterward."

Her heart skipped a beat. Matthew was handsome and likable, and he would make some lucky girl a wonderful sweetheart. He was nineteen while she was twenty-four. Despite the age difference, she gave serious consideration to having a relationship with him until the fact hit home again that James was his *bruder.*

If Matthew courted her and they became serious with the intention of marriage, then James would be her brother-in-law, and she would have to see him often. She was afraid that her feelings for James would complicate her future, and Matthew would be the one who would ultimately suffer. While she'd suspected Matthew's feelings for her, she'd never thought he would make them known.

"I appreciate the invitation, Matthew," she said gently, because the last thing she wanted to do was hurt this kind young man. "But I think I should stay in. I wouldn't feel comfortable at a singing. I'm sure my younger sisters, Meg, Ellie and Charlie, will be going, but I feel as if the time for singings has passed me by."

Although he hid it well, she could sense his disappointment. "I thought you might like to get out a bit, but I understand."

"Matthew Troyer, you're a nice man and a *gut* friend," she said sincerely.

He gazed at her a long moment before his expression warmed. "Not what I was hoping from you, but I'll take it." He stood. "I should get home. James is staying for supper. 'Tis late. I didn't want to wait until tomorrow to bring your kitten." He brushed off his pants, then extended a hand to help Nell up.

Nell accepted his help and wished that things could be different for them. If she hadn't loved Michael and then met James, she might have given their relationship a chance. She was aware of the warmth of his fingers about hers as he pulled her to her feet. He released her hand immediately and stepped back.

"*Danki*, Matthew."

His smile wasn't as bright as previously. "You're *willkomm*."

Nell accompanied him to his buggy. "Matthew—"

"'Tis fine, Nell." Genuine warmth filled his blue eyes. "At least we are friends, *ja*?"

"Always."

"I'll see you at church service."

"*Danki* for bringing the kitten."

He laughed. "'Twas my pleasure."

As she watched him leave, she realized what Matthew had revealed—that James was at Adam Troyer's residence for supper.

Nell sighed sadly. James had brought the kitten with him to his parents' house. Apparently, he realized how upset she'd been by their kiss, so he asked Matthew to bring her the kitten.

She closed her eyes as she was overwhelmed. True to form, James remained ever thoughtful of her feelings. What was she going to do about this?

Chapter Nine

"Will you be coming to church service?" *Mam* had asked James last night during Saturday evening's supper. He had come for dinner the night before when his family had convinced him to stay the weekend. Upset over how he'd chased Nell away with his kiss, he'd been in need of some cheering up. And his parents and siblings' love and acceptance of him always made him feel better. So he'd spent last night, and this morning he'd promised to stay another. Therefore, he wasn't surprised when his mother suggested that he attend Sunday services with them.

"*Mam*, I haven't been to church in years," he'd confessed.

"All the more reason to come."

James had gazed at his mother, seen the warmth and love in her brown eyes and smiled. "I'll come."

Sunday morning he went to the barn to see to the animals. As he walked, he glanced down at his garments. On Friday, when he'd been asked to stay, he'd wanted to retrieve his clothing from his apartment. His stepfather had said there was no need. James and he were the same size, and so was Matthew. They owned enough garments to get James through the weekend.

Which is how James found himself wearing Amish clothing for the first time since he'd turned eighteen and left the community. To his surprise, he realized that he felt comfortable in them. It was like putting on a favorite T-shirt. They fit him like a glove and felt good against his skin.

He'd gotten up early and spent longer in the barn than he needed to. But it had felt good spending time with his stepfather's horses and goats. Usually the only animals he saw were sick or in need of medical care, except for the ones that only needed their vaccines and their annual exams.

He'd enjoyed the smell of horse and hay and the sound of the animals shifting in their stalls. The simple joy of just standing and watching kept him longer than he should have been.

But when was the last time he'd spent any amount of time in his stepfather's barn? The moment of peace wouldn't last long, he knew, so he stayed to enjoy it until, conscious of the time, he hurried back to the house. He entered the kitchen just as his mother announced that breakfast was ready. He joined his family at the table and thoroughly enjoyed the home-cooked meal.

"We have to leave for service by eight thirty," Adam said.

"Where is it this week?" Matthew asked.

"The Amos Kings." Adam turned to James. "You've seen the new *schuulhaus*?"

"*Ja*, I know where it is."

"It's on the Samuel Lapp property. The Amos Kings live across the street."

"The large farm?" James murmured. James suspected that the man farmed for a living. Most members of the Amish community had smaller farms that provided food with only minimal cash crops. But he suspected that it was different with Amos King. His farm was larger than most in the area.

"*Ja*, Amos farms more than any of us. Samuel Lapp does some construction work for members of our community. He donated the property, and he with his sons built the *schuul*."

The school hadn't existed when James had lived here as a teenager. Back then, the school had been a small building in need of repair on the opposite side of town. James hadn't attended the school. Since he'd made the decision to become a veterinarian like his late father, his mother and stepfather had allowed him to attend public school.

"Do you have something I can borrow for church?" James asked. Amish dress for church was white shirt with black vest and black pants. He would have looked out of place in his Amish work clothes of a solid shirt, navy tri-blend pants and black suspenders. His mother left the room and returned within seconds. She carried a white shirt, black vest and black dress pants. She extended them to her son.

"I kept them in case you visited and needed them."

James felt his emotions shift as he accepted his former Sunday clothes.

"Danki, Mam," he said thickly. Emotion clogged his throat, making it difficult to swallow.

"Are you certain they will still fit?" Matthew asked.

"Matt."

"He's right, *Dat*. I'm a boy no longer. What if these don't fit?"

"Only one way to find out," Adam said.

James headed upstairs to change. To his amazement, the clothes fit as if tailor-made for him.

His mother smiled when he came downstairs wearing the garments. "I knew they'd fit."

"I don't have a hat," James said.

"*Ja*, you do," Matthew said. At *Mam's* insistence, Matthew must have retrieved the black felt hat James had in his youth.

James waited until he and his family were outside before he put it on.

Like the clothes, the hat fit perfectly.

"There you go. You've no worries. You look as Amish as the rest of us," *Mam* said.

James grinned. He couldn't help it. At one time, he'd objected to wearing Amish clothing, but now he appreciated how the simple garments made him feel as if he was a part of something big.

The first person James noticed as Adam steered his buggy onto the Amos King property was Nell Stoltzfus. He experienced a stark feeling of dismay as he saw that she was talking with a young handsome man closer in age to her than he was.

He knew he had no right to be upset. Despite their kiss, Nell and he didn't have a relationship. Given their life circumstances, they never would, but that knowledge didn't make the sight any easier for him.

Matthew jumped out as soon as the vehicle stopped. "Nell!" He hurried in her direction. *"Hallo!"*

James's heart ached as he climbed out more slowly and watched Matthew approach Nell. Unlike him, his brother hadn't hurt Nell or caused her discomfort and embarrassment.

He held out his hand to his sister Maggie. "That's the bishop," she told him as if she could read his mind. "His wife is over there." She gestured toward a chair in the sun. The woman looked frail as if she'd been ill.

"That's his wife?"

"*Ja*, Catherine. They have a two-year-old son, Nicholas. She's been under the weather recently, and we haven't seen much of her—or him. She must have felt well enough to come. If they leave right after services, then we know that she's not recovered as much as we'd like to think."

James met his sister's gaze. "And you're telling me this because…"

"Nell. I saw your face when you saw her with him, but you've no need to worry." Maggie studied him. "You know that she's a member of the church. Not like me and our siblings but as an adult member. She joined it five years ago, when they moved to Happiness after Meg recuperated from her illness."

"Young people don't normally join the church until right before marriage."

"*Ja*, that's true. But for some reason, Nell felt compelled to make the commitment. She can no longer leave the church without consequences."

James's stomach burned. "Being shunned by her family and community."

"*Ja*, James. She chose the path of the Lord when she was only nineteen. She'd had no sweetheart or prospects of marriage, but she made the choice anyway."

"I see." It was as bad as James had thought. There wasn't even the hope of a future with Nell, not with his life firmly entrenched in the English world while she lived happily within her Amish community.

"Nell!"

Nell turned and smiled. "*Hallo*, Matthew."

"Bishop John," Matthew greeted.

"Matthew."

"How is your wife?" he asked.

John gestured toward the woman seated in a chair in the backyard. "She wanted to come."

"That's *gut*. She must be feeling better."

The bishop eyed his spouse with concern. "*Ja*, she says she is."

But Nell could read his doubt.

"Where is Nicholas?" Matthew asked.

"Meg has him." She gestured toward the back lawn where the boy walked with her sister. "He's getting big, John. He's two, *ja*?"

"Almost three." The church elder smiled. "He's a *gut* boy. I can't imagine our lives without him."

"'Tis why the Lord blessed you with such a fine *soohn*."

Nell studied the small boy and wondered how difficult it must be for Catherine to care for him when she felt so ill. She had no idea what was wrong with John's wife, but she said a silent prayer that the woman would recover quickly.

"I'm going to check on Catherine," John said.

"If you need anything, please don't hesitate to let me know. I'll do what I can to help."

The bishop gave her a genuine smile. "*Danki*, Nell."

"How is the little one?" Matthew teased after John had left.

"You mean Naomi?"

"You named her!"

"Did you really think that I'd keeping calling her little one—or *kotz*?"

Matthew laughed. "Naomi, I like it."

"Like what?" Maggie said as she approached from behind. "*Hallo*, Nell."

"Maggie!" Nell greeted her with delight. She genuinely liked Maggie Troyer.

"I've brought someone with me." She stepped aside, and Nell found herself face to face with James.

She blushed and looked away. "James. Thank you for Naomi."

"Her kitten," Matthew explained.

A twinkle entered James's dark eyes. "I see. Do you like her?"

Nell stared. "What's not to like?"

His features became unreadable as he looked away.

She immediately regretted her behavior. "How is Joey?"

His face cleared and brightened. "He's doing well. Fred picked him up on Friday. I called to check on him yesterday. Joey's making great strides in his recovery."

"Any idea yet who hurt him?"

Maggie frowned. "Is this the little dog you were telling us about?" she asked her brother.

James nodded.

Matthew scowled. "Surely there is something that can be done."

"I called and reported it to the police. They're keeping an eye out. It's going to be hard because there are no witnesses to the crime."

Ellie approached. "'Tis time for service."

Immediately, everyone headed toward the King barn where benches had been set up in preparation for church. Nell entered and sat in the second row in the women's area. Maggie and Ellie slid in beside her and moments later, they were joined by Maggie's sisters Abigail and Rosie.

Nell watched as James took a seat in the men's area between Matthew and her cousin Eli Lapp.

Soon all of the men were seated in one area of the room while the women and children were in another.

The room quieted as Abram Peachy, the church deacon, and Bishop John Fisher, who saw that his wife was comfortably seated next to Nell's aunt Katie Lapp, approached the pulpit area. Preacher Levi Stoltzfus, a distant relative of her father's family, led the service by instructing everyone to open the *Ausbund* and sing the first hymn.

The service progressed throughout the morning as it usually did. Abram spoke to the congregation first, then they sang the second hymn before Levi began to preach. Bishop John had a few words of wisdom for the church community, then the service was declared officially over.

Nell was conscious of James seated across the room. Dressed in Amish Sunday best, he was handsome, his presence a strong reminder of what recently had transpired between them.

Soon, everyone left the barn to enjoy a shared meal provided by the community women. After helping to serve the men, Nell gravitated toward her family with her own plate of food.

"Did you get any of Miriam Zook's pie?" her *mam* asked. Nell shook her head. "You should try it before there's nothing left to taste."

Nell got up from her family's table. "Anyone want something while I'm up?"

"A glass of ice tea," *Dat* said.

She nodded. "Meg? Leah? Do you need anything to drink?"

"We have lemonade," Leah said. "*Danki*, Nell."

As she wandered over to the dessert and drink tables, Nell thought of James and wondered whether or not he'd left. She had her answer as she poured her father a glass of ice tea.

"Nell."

"James!" She nearly dropped the glass, but James quickly reached out to steady it.

"I need to talk with you."

"About what?" she said breathlessly.

"I wanted to apologize about the—"

"Don't say it," she gasped. "Please, James. Not here."

"Then will you understand if I just say that I'm sorry?"

"Ja," she said quickly and tried to dash away. But James followed her. "Nell."

She sighed as she faced him. *"Ja?"*

"I'm glad you like your kitten. I saw her and thought immediately of you."

"That was kind of you."

"I don't feel kind." He took off his black hat and ran his fingers through his short dark hair. His haircut was the only thing that reminded her that he wasn't Amish. In his current garments, James looked as if he could easily fit into her world. The knowledge that his appearance was just an illusion upset her.

"James, I have to go."

"I miss you, Nell," he said.

"Don't!" She didn't need to hear how much he'd missed her. Or to have to admit the truth that she'd missed him, too. Despite his Amish relatives and appearance, James was an *Englisher*, and she had to get over him. She couldn't allow herself to care.

Nell worked to shove thoughts of James from her mind as she hurried back to her family. The afternoon passed too slowly as she felt the continued tension of James's presence.

"You're quiet," Leah said beside her hours later as they rode home in their father's buggy.

"Just tired."

She felt her sister's intense regard and turned to smile at her reassuringly. To her relief, Leah seemed to accept her explanation. "At least, 'tis Sunday, and we can read or play games if we want."

"Ja." Nell made an effort to pull herself from her dark thoughts. She would enjoy their day of rest and try not to worry about tomorrow and her need to find an Amish husband fast before her father decided to find one for her. Or she did something she'd forever regret, like giving into her feelings for James.

That night, Nell prayed for God's help in finding a husband, in doing the right thing as a member of her Amish community. She pleaded with the Lord to help her get over the *Englisher* who'd stolen her heart and threatened her future happiness.

Chapter Ten

"You like James," Leah said as she cornered Nell in the barn Monday morning.

"*Ja*, he is a fine veterinarian. I respect him."

"*Nay*, Nell. You *care* for him." She paused. "You love him."

Nell felt a flutter in her chest as her denial got hung up in her throat. "Why would you think such a thing?"

"I saw the way you looked at him."

"What do you mean?" She felt a sharp bolt of terror. "I don't look at him in any certain way."

"And he looks at you in a certain way," Leah said, surprising her. "He cares for you."

But Nell was shaking her head. She didn't need the complication of a forbidden relationship with the *Englisher*.

"Nell, you should think about marrying. Has *Dat* mentioned it to you again?"

Nell brushed a piece of straw off her skirt. "Yesterday after we got home from church. I explained that I've been trying. I considered Matthew Troyer. I know he likes me, and he's a *gut* man, despite the fact that he is too young for me."

"He's not too young. Many of our women marry younger husbands."

"*Ja*, but their young husbands are not *bruders* to a man you are trying to forget."

"Ha!" Leah exclaimed. "So you *are* attracted to James!"

Nell nodded, feeling glum. "I can't help it. And he likes me, which makes it all the more difficult." She sighed. "I care for him, but 'tis hopeless." She put Naomi into her bed and stood. "Do you know *Dat* wanted me to think about marrying Benjamin Yoder? He moved to Happiness recently."

"Isn't he in his sixties?"

"*Ja*, but that isn't the worst of it. Benjamin came here from Indiana." She shuddered just thinking about the man. "I'm sure he's nice but, Leah, he's never been married. Or had children. I can't imagine…" She blushed. "And what if after he marries, he decides he wants to go home to Indiana? His wife would be expected to go with him. I don't want to leave Happiness. This is my home, and my family is here."

"You won't have to marry him. We'll find someone else for you first."

Nell smiled. "We?"

"I'll help you. We don't want to set a precedence of *Dat* choosing our husbands."

"And at twenty-one, you'll be the next *dochter* our *vadder* will want to see married and with children."

Leah inclined her head. "*Ja.* I'll find my own man, and I won't marry for anything other than love."

"And if you take too long and *Dat* wants to interfere?"

"You mean, help me along." Leah grinned. "Then I'll expect you to step in despite the fact that you'll be happily married to your chosen man with your seven children clinging to your apron strings."

"Seven!" Nell couldn't control a snort of laughter. "How long do you think *Dat* will be willing to wait for you? Certainly not long enough for me to give birth to seven *kinner*?"

Her sister shrugged. "Not to worry. 'Tis all just a thought anyway. You'll find your own husband, and I'll find mine."

"Where?"

"Look around. There are a lot of young men in our community."

"Men like Matthew," Nell murmured. "I already told you why I can no longer consider him."

"Because of James."

"Ja." She sighed. "If only I'd met James years ago, before I'd met Michael, then we might have had a chance."

"Michael?" Leah frowned. "Who is Michael?"

James unlocked the clinic Monday morning and went inside. He turned on the computer at the front desk, then slipped into his office to work while he waited for his staff. He made a list of patients he needed to check up on, and just as he finished, he heard the opening of the front door and Michelle's voice.

"Good morning, Dr. Pierce!" she called.

"Good morning, Michelle."

The young woman appeared in his doorway. "You don't look well. Don't tell me you caught the stomach bug, too?"

"No, I'm fine. Tired but fine."

"I'm sorry that I was out sick so long. I knew with Nell here that you'd be able to manage." She frowned. "Is Nell coming in today?"

He shook his head. "I don't need her now that you and Janie are back." It seemed a lie, telling Michelle that he didn't need Nell. But it was true that he didn't need her in the office. He needed—wanted—her in his personal life.

I shouldn't have kissed her, James thought when Michelle had settled in at the front desk. What on earth had he been thinking?

He hadn't been thinking. He only knew that at that moment he'd been unable to deny his growing feelings for her and he'd desperately needed that kiss.

A longing so sharp and intense that it made him groan and hang his head into his hands gripped him. He had a business to run, a goal to accomplish. It didn't matter how he felt about someone he had no right to love.

He straightened, threw back his chair and went to the window to enjoy the view of the farm across the road. He had done what he'd set out to do—become a veterinarian like his father.

James knew his father had never expected him to follow the same path, despite the fact that James had loved every moment he'd spent at his dad's side while his father had gone out on calls. James enjoyed his job, and he was sure John Pierce would be proud of the man he'd become and the vocation he'd chosen. But then, did he have moments like this when he'd felt empty inside?

He thought of his siblings. They were so happy and at peace with their lives. They didn't seem to be plagued by the same doubts and unrest that frequently overcame him lately. He felt torn between his chosen life and the life he'd left behind. Spending time with his family gave him a small measure of peace, something he hadn't experienced in a long time.

Suddenly he heard Janie in the treatment room, taking instruments out of the autoclave and putting them within easy reach. They had a full slate of appointments today.

His assistant appeared in his doorway. "Your first patient has arrived. She's new—Mrs. Simmons with her Siberian Husky, Montana. I've put them in room three."

He turned from the window. "Thank you, Janie." He took one last look at the fields of corn that grew thick and lush in the distance before he left his office to see his first patient.

Though everything went smoothly, the day seemed to drag on. James had seen three new patients who told him how pleased they were with his care of their pets. They would tell others about the clinic, each one had promised.

While he knew that was good news, he couldn't seem to get excited about it. His business was growing, which was what he wanted. But then why didn't he feel good or complete? Why did he keep thinking about his family and the life he could have had if he'd stayed within the community? Why couldn't he stop envisioning a different choice which could have given him what he needed and wanted most…a loving relationship with Nell Stoltzfus?

Janie approached him in the treatment room. "Dr. Pierce, I've cleaned the exam room and mopped the floors."

He glanced at her with surprise. His assistant had never cleaned the floors since she'd started work at the clinic. "Thank you, Janie."

"Is there anything else you need?" she asked.

James glanced at his watch. It was already well past closing time. "No, you've done enough, and I appreciate it. Go on home. I'll see you tomorrow."

The girl hesitated as if she had something to say. "Dr. Pierce?"

He looked at her with raised eyebrows. "Yes?"

She shook her head. "I just wanted to thank you for letting me take two weeks' vacation. It meant a lot to me. I know it couldn't have been easy for you while I was gone. Especially with Michelle out sick."

He smiled. "I managed to find some help. But I won't have to worry now that you're back."

"Good night, Dr. Pierce."

"James," he said. "Call me James. We've worked together long enough, don't you agree? Even Michelle calls me James."

Janie grinned. "Good night, James. I'll see you in the morning."

The office was quiet. He enjoyed the silence

after hours of tending to his noisy patients. Normally, he'd reflect on his day's work and experience satisfaction. But not today. In fact, he hadn't felt satisfied since the last day Nell had worked at the clinic.

He checked to ensure that the clinic was locked up before he headed home. The sun was bright in the sky, but it looked like there might be rain in the distance to the east. He would miss the longer daylight hours once fall came. The thought of staying alone in his apartment made him ache.

He felt a tightening in his chest that didn't go away as he reached his apartment and climbed up the stairs. By the time he entered his home, there was a painful lump in his throat and his tired eyes burned.

He threw his keys on the kitchen table, then collapsed onto his sofa. He stared at the ceiling, angry with himself for loving Nell—and for driving her not only out of his office but out of his life.

They could have remained friends if he'd controlled his growing feelings for her. But he'd had to go and kiss her—and ruin their friendship, the only thing he was permitted to have with her.

Four more days of work before the weekend. He had a standing invitation to stay at home. After long years away, he felt compelled to spend as much time on the farm as possible. It wasn't only his mother who was glad whenever he stayed. His stepfather, sisters and stepsiblings were happy to see him, too.

He knew Adam kept busy trying to keep up with his lawn furniture business. His stepfather had added children's swing sets to the list of items he could sell to his customers. If Adam would allow it, he'd like to help with the furniture. He was good with his hands and had learned from his stepfather when he was in high school. He could work with Adam on Saturdays unless he received an emergency call about a patient. He was busy at the clinic during the week and work was not allowed within the Amish community on Sundays.

He envisioned cutting wood, bolting long heavy boards together to form the legs of a swing set. It was something to look forward to—helping Adam with his business and on the farm.

James smiled and closed his eyes. And couldn't block the mental images of Nell that sprang immediately to mind. Only they weren't images of Nell walking away after he'd kissed her.

They were of her walking toward him on their wedding day.

Chapter Eleven

Nell pulled the buggy into the barnyard a little after one in the afternoon. She'd made beds, done the laundry and shopped for her mother. Instead of feeling as if she'd accomplished something, she felt totally out of sorts. Once again, she went to seek comfort from her animals, most particularly Jonas. When she'd returned from the store, she'd put away *Mam*'s groceries, then went directly to the barn.

Jonas greeted her enthusiastically, and she felt her mood lighten as she slipped inside his stall. His happy cries and kisses as she sat down beside him were just what she'd needed. Her fierce longing for a man she couldn't have upset her. She'd never expected to love again, and that she loved James made it hard.

She didn't know how long she sat playing with Jonas, but it must have been some time. Jonas finally exhausted himself and curled up to sleep in her lap. Nell studied him with a smile. Then her eyes filled with tears. It had been Jonas who had first brought her into contact with James Pierce.

Nell lay back against the straw and closed her eyes. It was how her sister Leah found her several minutes later.

"Nell."

She opened one eye. Leah's concerned expression wavered in her narrow vision. She opened her other eye and sat up. "Leah. I'm just having a rest."

Her sister regarded her with worry. "Are you ever going to tell me about Michael?"

Nell had put her sister off after she'd made the mistake of mentioning Michael's name. She'd had no intention of ever telling her family about him. Michael was dead, and there didn't seem to be any reason to resurrect her feelings for him—and her grief.

Jonas stirred in Nell's lap as Leah slipped inside and knelt in the stall beside her. "He's a *gut* dog." She reached to stroke the dog's fur.

Nell smiled. "He gives me comfort."

Leah looked at her. "Why did you need comfort? Because of Michael?"

Nell stiffened. "Leah…"

"You should just tell me. I won't tell anyone

if you don't want me to." Leah studied her with compassion. "What happened, Nell?"

Nell felt her face heat up.

"Nell—"

"James kissed me."

"What?"

"He kissed me. He didn't grab or hurt me. It was an innocent kiss that happened after we accidentally bumped heads."

"Nell," Leah whispered.

"Ja, I know. That's why I didn't go back to work for him at the clinic."

Leah eyed her with sympathy. "Although you loved the job."

"I only had one day left. Why should I risk it?"

As Leah remained quietly beside her, Nell finally gave in to the urge to tell her about Michael. "Leah, I've kept something from you and our family. It happened right before and then during the time Meg was ill."

Leah shifted to sit. "Michael?"

"Ja," Nell said. "He was an *Englisher*. I fell in love with him and we used to meet each night in secret. Our meetings were innocent, but he was handsome and kind, and I loved him."

Leah gazed at her with confusion. "Michael left you?"

"Not exactly. One night he asked me to marry him. I told him I would think about it, although

I knew what I was going to tell him the next day. That I would leave the community to be his wife."

Her sister frowned. "I don't understand."

"That night I waited for Michael, and he didn't show—it was the night that Meg became ill. I went to our special spot, ready to give him my answer. I knew he loved me, and when he didn't come, I thought he'd been detained for some reason. I waited for hours, then finally I went home. I went right to my room and cried and prayed and hoped that I hadn't been a fool for loving him."

Tears filled Nell's eyes, and she couldn't hold back a sob. "Then Meg got sick, and we all went to the hospital. I couldn't think about Michael, Meg needed me—she needed all of us."

"You were the strong one, and *Mam* and *Dat* needed you, too," Leah murmured, her blue eyes filled with emotion.

"The next day I was coming back to Meg's room after getting tea from the cafeteria, I heard a terrible loud beeping. It was in a room on the same floor as Meg's. I looked inside as I walked past and that's when I saw him. It was Michael, hooked up to life support.

"At first, I felt faint, but then I wanted to run to him. I needed to scream and cry and beg him to get better. I started into the room, but his nurse stopped me. She told me that I was in the wrong room, that Meg was in another. She said that this particular patient—Michael—wasn't allowed visitors." Nell wiped away tears. "The nurse looked at me and saw Amish. No one would have believed me if I'd told them we were in love."

She felt Leah's touch on her arm. "What happened to him?"

Nell's eyes filled with tears as she was overcome by her memories of that day. "I later learned that he'd been in a car accident. He was driving to meet me when a drunk driver struck him." She stood and turned away as her tears trailed down her cheeks.

She hugged herself with her arms. "Michael died from his injuries the next day. I wanted to rail against God, but in the end I put myself into His hands instead. I prayed for Meg to get well. I had already lost Michael, and I couldn't let myself grieve. I knew I'd fall apart and completely lose it. The only thing I could do was to pray for Meg's recovery."

Nell offered Leah a sad smile as she continued, "When Meg got better, I was so relieved. I'd made a promise to God, and I kept it. I joined the Amish church less than three months later."

Leah drew a sharp breath. "That's why you didn't wait until marriage. You'd lost the only man you'd ever love—or so you thought, and you thanked the Lord for Meg's recovery by fulfilling your promise to Him."

"Ja," Nell whispered. Her tears trickled unchecked. With a cry of sympathy, Leah hugged her. "Leah, you can't tell anyone. Please. You can't tell *Dat* or *Mam* or our sisters. Meg especially must never know."

Leah opened her mouth to object.

"Please, Leah."

"I promise that I won't tell them, but only if they don't ask. If one of them learns the truth, I won't lie."

She released a sharp breath. Nell was sure that after all of this time no one would find out. *"Danki."*

"But now you're in love with the *English* veterinarian. But this time the choice of whether or not to leave is no longer yours."

Nell inclined her head. *"Ja,* 'tis not."

"You've joined the church, and there is no obvious way for you and him to be together."

"Ja."

Leah stood abruptly, held out her hand and pulled Nell to her feet. "You've done the right thing. Avoiding him."

"But it still hurts."

"I know," Leah said. "Come. Let's go into the *haus*. It's near suppertime, and you must be famished."

Nell stared at her sister. She had no idea that

by simply telling Leah about Michael she'd feel a lightening of her burden. "I *am* hungry."

Leah grinned. "Let's hurry in before our younger sisters decide to eat everything and leave us nothing."

When they entered the kitchen, it was to find their other three sisters and their mother working together to prepare a meal.

"Nell, I wondered where you'd gone to," *Mam* said. "*Danki* for doing the wash and all the housework."

"I didn't mind. I like being busy."

Her brow furrowing, *Mam* glanced her way. If she'd noticed Nell's red-rimmed eyes, she didn't mention it. "How's your kitten, Naomi?"

"She's fine. *Dat* was *gut* about allowing me to keep her."

"Because he knows that you won't leave her care to your sisters, and you prefer to take care of her yourself."

Dat came in when the meal was ready. He gave the prayer of thanks. Conversation during dinner was loud and filled with feminine laughter. Nell smiled at Ellie as she regaled them with a story about the one family she cleaned for. Meg offered comments on how Ellie should handle the husband the next time he left food on dirty dishes on his night table.

Nell became aware of her father's gaze as

Charlie joined in with the outrageous solution of putting the food in the man's bed and the dishes in his bathtub. As her father watched her, she saw something in his eyes that gave her concern.

"I'll lose my job if I do that." Ellie laughed.

"Husband," *Mam* addressed him. "Chocolate cake for dessert?"

Dat nodded to *Mam,* a soft expression on his face.

Once the leftover fried chicken was put away, *Mam* brought out the cake and sliced each of them a nice-sized piece. When they were done with dessert, Nell and her sister Leah rose to clear the supper dishes while Charlie and Meg filled up the sink basin and started to wash. With five daughters in the house, there was always plenty of help, so when her father beckoned to her, Nell did whatever any good daughter would do. She handed Ellie her dish towel and followed him out into the other room.

She felt edgy as she waited for her father to speak. She had a feeling she knew what he wanted to talk about.

"Have you given it any thought?"

"It?"

"Marriage. A husband." Her father studied her thoughtfully.

She relaxed and smiled. *"Ja, Dat.* I haven't

found the man I want to marry yet, but I will. I just need a little more time."

Dat sighed. "You can have more time, but not too much." Then he hesitated as if he had something else on his mind. "Nell, I know how much you enjoy your animals. You've got a certain way with them, everyone says so. But you have to face the fact that your husband might not care for them as you do."

Nell gazed at him with a little smile on her lips. "Then I'll find a man who does love animals as much as I do."

He narrowed his gaze. "You're asking a lot of the man who hasn't married you yet."

"I'll find the right man, and he'll understand how I feel."

"You need to find him quickly, *dochter*."

"How can I rush this? I'll not marry for anything but love."

Her father's jaw tightened. "Are you disrespecting me with your tone, girl? I'm still your *vadder*."

She sighed. "*Dat*, I mean no disrespect. But this isn't easy for me. I thought I might be a *schuul* teacher until I meet a man I can love and who loves me, too."

"'Tis past the time to be thinking about becoming a *schuul* teacher. 'Tis time you took a husband."

"You think I have nothing to offer the *kinner*?" she asked softly. She was hurt by his dismissal of her skills. Was she that old that all he could think of was marrying her off?

"You could still marry Benjamin Yoder. He's single and never been married."

"*Nay!* I'll not marry a man older than my own *vadder*!"

Her father swallowed. "In truth, I don't want that for you either."

"I didn't think you wanted me to be unhappy."

His lips firmed. "Of course, I want your happiness. 'Tis my fondest hope that all of my girls will be happy in marriage, but time is passing you by, Nell. You have to take your chance soon."

Tears filled her eyes, and she tried to blink them away. She thought of Michael and then James. She could love James, marry him if he were a member of the Amish community. James loved animals as much as she did. Her heart ached, for she knew she would never have a life with him.

"Nell…" Her father's expression softened. "Know this. I do want you to be happy."

"*Ja*, I know."

"You deserve to have a husband, a family. You'll make a wonderful *mudder*."

"*Dat,* I'll try harder to find someone I can

love. But *please* don't arrange a husband for me. I can't...*please*."

He nodded. "You will be open-minded? Give up this notion of being a *schuul* teacher?"

"Ja, Dat."

The man looked relieved. *"Gut."* He smiled. "How is Jonas?" he said, quickly changing the subject. The little dog had worked his way into her father's heart, it seemed.

"He's doing well. Have you been to visit him?"

A slight tide of red crept into her father's cheeks. "This morning."

"He's a wonderful pet." Nell gazed at her father with fascination. "And Naomi? Have you visited with her, too?"

He looked embarrassed. "Neither one works or provides a service," her father pointed out.

"Ja, they do. They give unconditional love."

Her father laughed. "That they do, so I guess that is something."

Friday morning, James woke up with a stiff neck, a sore back and with the television murmuring softly. He must have finally fallen asleep on the sofa and left it on. Unable to sleep for hours last night, he'd alternately stared at the ceiling and the TV.

He couldn't get Nell out of his mind. How could he have been so foolish to give into his feelings? If he had controlled himself, he might have been able to spend more time with her.

He glanced at the clock on the cable box: 6:45 a.m. He had to get moving, or he'd be late for work. He sat up quickly and groaned at his aching muscles. There were consequences for sleeping on his old sofa five nights in a row. He'd fallen asleep to the noise from the TV, so tired each night that he'd been unable to find the strength to go to bed.

He grabbed the remote and turned off the TV. For a moment, his apartment was blissfully silent. He closed his eyes and drank the quiet in.

But then his thoughts filled with Nell again, and his brain buzzed with regret. James stood and headed to get ready for work. The only bright side was that it was the weekend, and he'd be spending it with his family. And there was a possibility that he might see Nell again on Sunday.

When he saw her, he vowed, he wouldn't joke or smile or cause her discomfort. He would be polite so that she didn't feel threatened. He wanted her in his life, even if only from a distance.

"James?" Janie poked her head into his office where he'd sat down between appointments. "Your next patient is here."

"Who is it?"

"Mrs. Becker and her dog Melly."

"Thank you. Would you please put them in exam room two?"

She nodded and left. James sat a moment longer.

The day went by quickly, for he had enough patients to keep him busy. He'd seen a record number of patients this week.

Janie was cheerful and clearly happy to be back at work in the clinic, but she wasn't Nell. Still, the tech's mood became infectious, and there were moments during that day that he smiled and laughed. Maybe he could do this after all, James thought. Maybe he could get past his feelings for Nell even if he couldn't ever forget her.

But then right before closing, Nell came to his office.

"Hi," he heard Janie say. "Welcome to Pierce Veterinary Clinic. Oh, poor baby, is this the little one who needs medical attention?"

He became alert as he heard Nell's voice, but he couldn't make out her words. He waited patiently for his assistant to come for him, although he was eager to see Nell and help.

"Come on back to exam room one," he heard Janie say. "You'll find it on the left as you go down the hall."

James had to smile. Nell knew exactly where the exam room was, where everything was in the clinic, but he doubted that Nell would say anything about having worked here while Janie was on vacation.

Janie entered his office. "You've a patient in exam room one. A little dog with a bee sting."

James was instantly concerned. Jonas got stung? He hurried into the exam room, where he found Nell with Jonas in her lap. She was hugging her pet against her. The dog was whimpering, and Nell was doing her best to soothe and comfort him. She must have sensed his presence because she looked up, happy to see him.

"James!" She rose quickly, mindful of her dog. "Jonas got stung by a bee. I put vinegar on it. I didn't know what else to do."

"You did good, Nell," he said quietly. "Vinegar helps draw out the toxin." He softened his expression as he held out his arms.

Nell didn't hesitate to hand him Jonas, and James experienced a deep sense of joy that she trusted him.

"Let's see, Jonas," he murmured as he placed him on the metal exam table in the room. "What have you done to yourself?" He examined his little swollen nose.

He heard Nell sniff, glanced over and saw her tears. "I only let him outside for a moment," she told him, "and I kept him on his leash."

"Nell," he said kindly, "dogs get into things. If they didn't, there wouldn't be a need for veterinarians like me." He used a magnifying glass to study the dog's nose more closely. "Ah, I see the stinger."

He reached into his pants pocket for his wallet. He flipped open the billfold and removed out a credit card.

He leaned close and scraped across the tip of Jonas's nose with the edge of the plastic card. "Got it!" he exclaimed. He displayed the tiny black object on his thumb. "Bee stinger." He smiled. "He should recover quickly." He handed her a tube of ointment. "For the itch," he said. "He's liable to keep scratching at his nose before it heals completely." He opened a bottle and shook out a pink pill. "Benadryl. And make sure you use the plastic collar I'm going to give you. He will try anything to get at his nose."

Nell nodded, and he knew that she recognized the bottle from her time working here. "I'll give him a Benadryl now. It doesn't appear that he's allergic, but I'll send you home with the liquid form anyway. It may help with some minor reactions. If his nose starts to swell or he becomes lethargic on the Benadryl, please bring him back. Better yet, call me immediately." He jotted his number on a Post-it note. "It's my cell phone. Don't wait if there's a change in him. All right?" He locked gazes with her.

"Ja," she promised, and he felt something tight ease within his chest.

Janie called out that she was finished for the day and was getting ready to lock up. He went to the door with Jonas in his arms to acknowledge his assistant's departure. "We'll be leaving in a minute. Good night, Janie. See you on Monday."

"James, *danki* for seeing him at such short notice," Nell said as he brought Jonas back to the table.

"Always," he said as he grabbed a collar from a cabinet and handed it to her. "Whenever you have a problem with Jonas or Naomi or any of your animals, come right in. You don't have to call. You don't need an appointment. Just come."

He saw her mouth open and close as she tried to process what he'd said. He watched her physically gather her composure. *"Danki."*

He glanced down at Jonas and smiled. "Back to your *mam*," he murmured as he lifted the little dog and placed him into Nell's waiting arms. His arm brushed Nell's, and for a moment, their eyes locked and tension arced between them.

He headed toward the door, waiting for her to follow him. "If he is still bothered by the sting, try using a cold pack on his nose. You can use ice in a plastic bag. Put it on his nose for short time intervals—about ten minutes on and fifteen off."

He opened the door. "Make sure it's not too cold for him. If it is, wrap the bag in a dish towel."

He gestured for Nell to precede him into the front reception area. "Take care of yourself, Nell—and Jonas."

"James, I need to pay you."

"Not necessary." His tone was insistent but gentle. "I still owe you for your help here in the office."

Nell sighed. "I… *Danki*."

He smiled and waited while she went out the door. Then he quickly closed it behind her before he called out to her or did something that he would regret. Like kiss her or hug her.

When she was gone, James locked up the office and drove to his family farm. Fifteen minutes later, he took a duffel bag from his trunk and headed toward the house. He entered through the kitchen.

"Hallo, Mam."

"James!" she gasped with pleasure. "It's late. I thought you'd changed your mind about spending the weekend."

"Not a chance. I had a late appointment." After setting his bag by the door, he pulled out a kitchen chair and sat down.

Her brow creased with concern. "Everything *oll recht*?"

"Dog with a bee sting. I was able to get out the

stinger. I was concerned because he got stung on the nose, but I believe he'll be fine."

His mother looked relieved, and something startling occurred to him. "*Mam*, how many times did Dad talk with you about his patients?"

Mam smiled. "Quite a few. He needed to talk, and I liked listening to him." She opened a cabinet door and pulled out two cups. "Coffee or tea?"

"Tea, please." He'd always found comfort in tea whenever he was sick or wanted to remember his time at home. His mother didn't say anything as she put on the kettle and took cookies out of the pantry. She set them within James's reach and then fixed their tea.

"What about dinner?" James asked.

"There's time. I was going to have tea myself," she assured him as she sat down across from him.

She prepared her tea the way she liked it, took a sip, then looked at him.

"Tell me what's wrong." Her warm brown eyes held concern.

"Nothing that can be fixed." He swallowed hard. "But I feel better now that I'm here."

Her expression grew soft. "James, this will always be your home. I love that you enjoy being here. Come whenever you want. You don't have to ask first."

James realized he'd said the same thing to Nell about the office. And he'd meant it. He smiled at his mother as a huge burden was lifted from his shoulders. *"Danki."*

He glanced toward the kitchen window as they finished their tea. "I parked behind the barn."

"Don't want anyone to know you're here, *ja*?" *Mam* teased.

"It doesn't seem right to park a car in your driveway."

She shook her head but a smile played about her mouth. "'Tis fine. You can park it wherever makes you feel better."

James reached out to clasp his mother's hand. "I love you, *Mam*," he said.

"I love you, *soohn*. I wish I could help with whatever is bothering you."

"You already have, *Mam*," he whispered.

"You'll be staying in Matt's room again," *Mam* said as he stood and retrieved his duffel.

He didn't mind. He and Matthew had become close since he'd moved back to Happiness. His brother seemed to enjoy his weekly visits almost as much as he enjoyed staying the weekends in his parents' house.

He carried his belongings upstairs and into Matthew's room which had two single beds. He put the duffel bag on the bed he'd been given the last time, then moved to look through the window at the farm fields below.

The crops Adam had planted were green and

thriving. James smiled. He enjoyed the view. It brought back childhood memories of living in Ohio with his parents and of his home here in Pennsylvania with his mother and stepfather.

"Come downstairs after you get settled," *Mam* called up. "You can keep me company while I make dinner. *Dat* and Matt are at your *onkel* Aaron's. Maggie, Abigail and Rosie have gone to the store but will be home soon. They'd planned to stop to see the Stoltzfus girls on their way back."

James felt a jolt. He wasn't surprised that his sisters knew the Stoltzfus girls. They belonged to the same Amish church community. But he hadn't realized that the girls were friendly.

Seeing Nell in his office this afternoon, knowing that she'd come to him for help, warmed him. He couldn't have Nell Stoltzfus as his sweetheart, but perhaps there was still hope that they could be friends.

His stepfather and brother arrived home an hour later, surprised to discover that James had gone to the barn to check on the animals.

"James!" Adam exclaimed. "*Gut* to see you again, *soohn*." He grinned. "Can't manage to stay away from us, *ja*?"

"Ja," James said soberly. "I enjoy spending the weekends with you." He swallowed. "If it's not too much trouble."

"You can stay every weekend—and every weekday if you'd like. We love having you here." He narrowed his gaze. "Where is your car?"

"Behind the barn." James spied his stepbrother, Matthew behind his father. "Matt, I hope you don't mind sharing again."

Matthew grinned. "I don't mind as long as you keep to your own side of the room."

James grinned. "You always know how to put me in my place, little *bruder*."

"As you know how to put me in mine, big *bruder*," he teased.

"Our animals *oll recht*?" Adam asked.

"They are fine." He met Adam's gaze. "They look well fed and healthy." He paused. "Are you having any problems with any of them?" Adam shook his head. *"Gut."*

"We're going inside," his stepfather said. "Coming?"

"Ja, Mam has a *gut* supper simmering on the stove. Chicken potpie." James regarded his brother with amusement. "You staying behind?"

"And have you eat my share of supper?" Matthew smiled. *"Nay."*

"You don't seem upset to have a roommate again," he told Matthew as they followed their father toward the house.

Matthew shrugged. "I've gotten used to you."

"Ja?" James smiled.

"You grew on me. It seems I've missed my older *bruder*," he confessed.

"*Danki*, Matt," James said softly. "I've missed you, too."

"Are you hungry?"

"Starved." James stared at his brother's garments. "I've brought my own clothes, but may I borrow some of yours?"

"Missing our suspenders, are you?" Adam teased. He turned to his other son. "Matthew, do you think you could find some clothes for your *bruder*?"

Matthew sighed. "If I must." But then he grinned. "I'm sure I have a few things that will fit him despite the fact that he's an old man now."

"Don't be smart, youngster," James said with a laugh. "I'm not an old man, and you know it."

James changed into the Amish garments that Matthew got out for him. He was standing with his brother by the pasture fence when his sisters arrived home with their purchases and news from Whittier's Store.

"Did you see Nell and Charlie?" Matthew asked.

"*Nay*, we didn't have time to stop. We saw Daniel and Isaac Lapp, and we got to talking with them. I wanted to give Leah some quilting fabric. I'll have to bring it with us tomorrow." Maggie glanced at her older brother. "Nice to see you at home again, *bruder*."

"Nice to be home again, Mags."

His sister growled playfully at his use of the *English* nickname.

"Supper!" their mother called.

"We'd best hurry. She may be needing help before we sit down to eat," Maggie said.

The sisters rushed on ahead of them, and the men followed. James felt an infusion of good humor. It was good to be home.

Nell's sisters were laughing. The five of them were in their family buggy taking a drive to visit their cousins.

Aunt Katie and Uncle Samuel would be hosting Visiting Sunday, and the girls wanted to help out in any way they could. With seven sons, more than half of whom were married, and Hannah, her eight-year-old daughter, Aunt Katie had less help than their *mam* did in the Stoltzfus house. Nell knew that Katie's daughters-in-law had offered to come, but they had children to take care of, and Katie thought it best if they stayed with her grandchildren. It was only natural for the Stoltzfus sisters, Katie's nieces, to help out instead.

Nell, who sat in the front passenger seat while Leah steered the horse, heard laughter from her sisters in the seat behind them. She glanced back. "Charlie, I don't know why you insisted on bringing Jonas. You don't have to watch him. His nose is fine. What will we do with him while we work?"

"I brought his kennel," Charlie said with a chuckle. "Stop, Jonas!"

"Nell, he's trying to give puppy kisses," Meg said with laughter.

"Trying and succeeding," Ellie said. "I just got licked in the face."

"Eww!" Meg said, and she roared with delight when she received a doggy kiss of her own.

"Look!" Charlie reached over Nell's shoulder to point to a farmhouse on the right. "There's Matthew Troyer. He's waving to us."

Nell glanced over with a smile that promptly froze on her face when she saw the man standing beside Matthew. She knew immediately who wore the Amish solid shirt and tri-blend denim pants with black suspenders. It was James. "Who's with him?" Ellie asked. Her voice held interest.

"You've met him," Meg said.

A car came up from behind them, and Leah slowed the buggy, steering it closer to the side of the road.

"'Tis Matthew's *bruder*, and he's someone too old for you," Charlie told her.

"Ha! As if any eligible man in our community

is too old for me," Ellie said. "He may be too old for you, Charlie, but not for me."

Nell couldn't keep her eyes from James. Her heart thumped hard as she recalled her time with Jonas in his office yesterday afternoon. He'd been kind and patient...and too professional.

Matthew leaned in to say something to his companion, and James turned, giving Nell a full view of his handsome features. The shock of her continued attraction to him hit her hard. It didn't matter if he'd been professional and friendly. As she met his gaze, she immediately recalled their kiss.

As if sensing Nell's disquiet, Leah looked over and frowned.

"James," Nell murmured. She gestured toward the man in Amish dress, and her sister's eyes widened.

Matthew waved at them to pull into the driveway. She and Leah exchanged glances. They had come for fabric. She could get it from Maggie and then leave immediately. Nell felt her pulse race as Leah turned on the blinker, then pulled onto the Troyers' dirt driveway.

"*Hallo*, Nell," Matthew greeted with a smile.

"Matthew," she greeted pleasantly. She flashed James a look. "James."

"Where are you headed?" the younger brother asked.

"Aunt Katie's," Leah said. "But Maggie has

some fabric that she was going to drop off today if she had the time."

"I'll get her for you," Matthew offered, drawing Nell's attention. She looked away as he entered the house, leaving the sisters alone with James.

"Will you be coming to visit at the Lapps tomorrow?" Charlie asked from the backseat.

"I don't know yet," James said.

Nell locked gazes with him. "You should come," she urged and was rewarded by his look of surprise.

"I'll consider it if my family goes," he said.

Nell blushed and was unable to look away.

Matthew exited the house with his sister.

"Sorry we didn't stop by this afternoon," Maggie said as she handed Nell a plastic bag.

"We could have gotten them from you tomorrow, but since we were on our way to Aunt Katie's anyway…"

After their initial eye contact, James seemed to be avoiding Nell's gaze.

There was no logical reason why she should feel hurt, Nell realized. Unless it was because, wrong or right, she wanted his attention.

"We should go—" Leah began.

Nell took the hint. "*Ja*, we need to go. It was *gut* to see you," she said. She started to turn away until James called out to her.

"Nell?"

She froze then glanced back.

"May I speak with you a moment?"

She nodded and followed him to where they could talk privately. "Is something wrong?"

James gazed at her warmly, his intense focus making her wish for things she couldn't have. He didn't say anything for a long moment, as if he were happy just to have her attention.

"James?"

His gaze dropped briefly to her mouth. "How's Jonas?" he asked.

She swallowed hard. "He's fine. Doing well. *Danki.*"

"Nell, I miss you."

"James, we can't do this. *I* can't do this."

"What exactly is this?" he asked quietly. "The fact that we like each other but shouldn't?"

"*Ja*, we shouldn't," she said and started to turn.

He captured her arm. "Nell, I'm sorry. I know I have no right to ask anything of you, but please… consider us being friends if we can't be anything more."

"I don't know if I can," she whispered.

"Can't be friends?"

"'Tis too risky. I want more, but it will never happen. So I'm sorry, James, but we can't be friends. Ever." With that last remark, Nell hurried back to the buggy where her sisters were chatting with Maggie and Matthew while they waited. Nell saw that their sister Abigail had joined them.

"*Hallo*, Abigail," she greeted, then she leaned into her sister and said, "Leah, we have to go. *Now*."

"Matthew, it was nice to see you," Nell said with a smile. "Nice to see you again, James," she said politely. She drew on all of her skills to hide the fact that she remembered his kiss and how much she'd enjoyed it. "Enjoy your time with your family."

James looked at her. "I will. *Danki*, Nell."

Leah climbed into the front seat of the carriage while Nell got in on the passenger side.

"Have a *gut* evening," Leah said.

"Bye, Nell," Matthew said. "I hope to see you at the Lapps' tomorrow."

Nell nodded. She had no choice but to go. Would James be there, as well?

Her glance slid over him briefly before she stared ahead as Leah steered their buggy toward Aunt Katie's. She shouldn't want him there, but she did. Nell closed her eyes. She was a fool for loving him. But she couldn't seem to help herself.

She needed to find an Amish husband…soon.

Chapter Twelve

Katie Lapp came out of the house as Leah steered the family buggy into the barnyard and parked. Nell climbed out and waited for Leah while their sisters ran toward the Lapp farmhouse.

"We've come to help, *Endie* Katie," Charlie cried.

"Wunderbor, g'schwischder dochter." *Wonderful, niece*, they heard their aunt exclaim. "I'm so glad you could come—all of you! Come inside!"

Leah hitched up the horse before she turned to Nell. "What are you thinking?"

Nell frowned. "I'm wondering why I can't forget him. He makes it hard, staying with his Amish family, dressing like them."

"He's still an *Englisher*, don't forget. He made the choice to leave our way of life." Leah fell into step beside her as they slowly made their way to the house.

"I know."

"But you still love him."

Nell met her sister's gaze with tears in her eyes. *"Ja."*

Why doesn't he wear jeans? Nell thought. He could have worn jeans, and she'd be unable to forget that he was *English* and unavailable to her. But would it have helped even to see him like that?

Nay, she thought. James in jeans was just as devastating to her peace of mind. Although seeing James in Amish clothes gave her a fierce longing for something she could never have.

Nell preceded Leah into Katie Lapp's house. *"Endie* Katie. Where would you like us to start?"

"Charlie and Hannah are in the kitchen. It would be helpful if you could work in the great room?"

"We'll start there then," Leah said.

Grabbing cleaning supplies and a broom, the sisters entered the large great room, where the family often gathered for late evening and Sunday leisure time.

"What are you going to do about your feelings for him?" Leah asked as she dusted the furniture.

"What can I do? 'Tis not like it matters one way or another how I feel. I have to marry within the Amish faith." Nell swept the floor with long, even strokes of the corn broom.

"You're upset," her sister pointed out. "And hurt. I don't know how to help you."

Nell blinked to clear her vision. There was suddenly a lump in her throat. "No one can help me."

"Matthew cares for you," Leah said. "You could still marry him."

"*Nay!* He'll still be James's *bruder.* And it will seem as I'm deliberately trying to hurt him."

"Matthew?"

"*Nay,* James."

"If he's staying the weekend, James may come visiting tomorrow."

"I know." Nell felt a burning in her stomach. Odds were that he'd come.

"There will be plenty of opportunities to have a word with him and clear the air." Leah paused in her dusting and touched her arm to draw her gaze. "You could check on *Onkel* Samuel's farm animals. 'Tis possible he'll follow you."

It was true. He might follow her because of the nature of his profession. "And if he does, what am I supposed to say to him that I haven't already said?"

"You'll think of something."

"You're not afraid I'll do something terrible, like run away and marry him?"

Her sister's blue eyes widened. "You're not actually considering it, are you?"

Nell's face heated. *"Nay."*

"Then we have nothing to worry about. Just tell him to leave you alone and be done with it."

Nell doubted that it would be so easy. She loved James too much to be cruel. But being cruel might be the only way for him to get on with his life without her.

James liked working side by side with Adam and Matthew. The manual labor on the farm felt good, and it gave him an outlet for the frustration of struggling to make a success of his practice. He also enjoyed helping Adam in his small furniture shop attached to the barn.

The only concession he allowed himself during these weekends was to keep his cell phone with him. He needed to take calls in the event of an emergency. Fortunately, there had been no such calls.

His thoughts focused on Nell as they did often during each day. The image of the young Amish woman constantly hovered in his mind. He'd seen her this afternoon, and he missed her already.

He sighed. There was no chance for them. Why couldn't he put her out of his mind?

Then there was Matthew. It was clear that his younger brother had feelings for Nell. It would be acceptable for Matthew and Nell to have a life together. Acceptable to the community, but not to him.

He heard a bell from the direction of the house.

"Dinnertime," Adam announced, glancing toward his sons who were fixing the fencing on the far side of the property.

"Thanks be to *Gott*. I'm as hungry as a bear." Matthew straightened and leaned on his shovel. The two brothers had just replaced a rotten fencepost.

"You're always hungry," *Dat* said.

"How do you know about a bear's appetite?" James teased. "They hibernate through the winter and don't eat while they're sleeping in their den."

"The animal expert," Matthew groused, but the grin on his face told James that he was teasing back.

"Wonder what *Mam's* fixed for supper?"

"More than you eat on your own, James, I'm certain."

James stretched, reaching over his head until he experienced the sharp pull of his arm muscles. He felt good, better than he had in a long time.

"Thanks—I mean, *danki* for allowing me to stay the weekend again," James said, regarding the two men beside him with warmth.

"Come every weekend. I'm always happy to share the work," Matthew joked.

Adam gazed at him with affection. "We enjoy having you, *soohn*."

The dinner bell resounded again, and the three men started toward the house.

"You want to see my place?" James asked his brother. "I live over Mattie Mast's Bakery."

"You do?" Matthew's eyes had widened. "Must smell *gut* in your *haus*."

"Most days. Monday through Saturday, it's a sure bet. I particularly like Tuesday's when Mattie makes her special chocolate cake."

"*Mam* made a chocolate cake this morning," Matthew said.

"She did?" The thought made his mouth water.

"She said something about it being your favorite," Adam interjected.

James suddenly felt emotional. "It is."

Adam regarded him with a knowing look.

Matthew, on the hand, appeared puzzled. "*Ja.* Why are you surprised?"

"I haven't been home much these last years." James paused. "I haven't been the best son."

"You're a fine *soohn*, James, and don't you forget it. As for not coming to visit much, you're home now, and you moved to Lancaster County to be closer to us, *ja*?" Adam said.

James nodded.

"Then stop fretting. Be welcome. Come and stay anytime you want. Move in if you'd prefer. We love having you here." He hesitated.

"Thank you, *Dat*," he said softly.

"Let's eat," Matthew rumbled. "I'm as hungry as a b-boar!"

James laughed, and Adam joined in. Matthew glanced at each of them sheepishly until he began to giggle himself.

They could smell *Mam's* cooking through the kitchen window. It was a warm day. In sweltering temperatures, the shades would be drawn and windows might be open or closed depending on whether or not there was a breeze.

James entered the house, stepping into the kitchen behind Adam and Matt. One look at the table laden with an Amish feast made everything worth it. He had missed such meals with his family. From the pleased look on her face as she noted his happiness, his mother had missed having him home, too.

Sunday morning Nell woke up early. The rest of the family was sleeping in. Since it was Visiting Day, they didn't have to be at the Lapps' until nine thirty or ten o'clock. She slipped downstairs, taking extra care to be quiet, and went into the barn to feed and water the animals.

Nell heard Jonas's excited barks. She hurried to his stall with a smile.

"*Hallo*, little one. Would you like to go outside?" She snapped on his leash and led him out of the barn. She walked about the property for a while, then took him back inside. Her gaze settled on Naomi's bed, and Nell was overwhelmed with sudden tears. James had known just what she would want—something for her new cat.

She crouched down and picked up Naomi. She was so tiny. The kitten was eating well, no doubt because James knew exactly what her cat would need. She grabbed a little toy, held it to Naomi's mouth. The kitten batted at the stuffed mouse playfully.

Nell put her down and watched for several moments, feeling a longing so intense that it nearly stole her breath. James. Why did she have to fall in love with an *Englisher*?

Nell was sure that Leah was correct. James was an *Englisher* with a stepfather, mother and siblings who were Amish.

She knew that she would have to talk with him, no matter how hard it would be to listen, and to step back after they'd parted friends.

She didn't want to be friends with James, but it was her only option. She poured dog food into Jonas's bowl and refilled his water dish.

James and she had a lot in common. They both loved animals. They enjoyed each other's company and got along well. But the most vital thing that was different about them was their chosen way of life.

Nell had chosen God's way through the Amish

church, while James had made the choice to leave the community and become a veterinarian, with a life with TV, radio, cars and computers. She couldn't help the small smile that formed on her lips. *Maybe not computers.* He didn't like using the one in the office. He left that up to Michelle to handle.

I'm sorry. His words came back to haunt her. What exactly had he been apologizing for? She'd thought it had been because of the kiss, but what if it was more?

Her mind replayed every day since her first meeting with James. From his tender care of Jonas, his compassion and concern for Joey, his patience and intensity while caring for Buddy and the other animals he treated in and outside of the practice. She sat, stroking Jonas, watching Naomi play, giving equal attention to both her beloved pets.

"Nell!"

"In here, Charlie!"

"We made breakfast. How long have you been out here?"

Nell shrugged. "What time is it?"

"Nine thirty."

She felt a jolt. "It is?" How had three hours passed so quickly? Had she been so wrapped up in her thoughts of James and what she was going to say to him that the minutes had flown by?

"*Ja*, come and eat. *Mam* and *Dat* will want to be heading to Aunt Katie's soon. There are muffins and pancakes, ham and bacon—and cereal if you want it."

"I'll be right there." Nell pushed to her feet. "Bye, little ones," she whispered.

Charlie waited for her outside the barn. "Who do you think will come visiting at *Endie* Katie's today?"

"I have no idea. The Kings and the Hershbergers, most likely."

"And the Masts and Troyers."

"And all their children and spouses and their grandchildren," Nell added.

"I wonder if the boys will play *der beesballe*."

"What else will they do on a nice summer's day?"

"*Ja*, they'll play baseball, and I'll get to watch." A mischievous look entered Charlie's expression. "Maybe I'll convince them to let me play."

Nell laughed and hugged her sister before they climbed up the front porch. "I have no doubt you'll be playing baseball today. You are *gut* at convincing people to do what you want."

Charlie paused and frowned. "Is that a bad thing?"

"*Nay*, sister, 'tis a *gut* thing," Nell said as they entered the house.

* * *

He wasn't here. The Troyers had arrived an hour ago, and there was no sign of James. Nell stood at the fence railing and overlooked her uncle's pasture.

I should have stayed and talked longer with him at the Troyers' yesterday.

But she hadn't. She'd become upset at seeing him there, at him being Matthew's brother, that she'd been eager to get away. And just when she'd made up her mind to tell him to leave her alone, he didn't show.

Nell heard laughter behind her. Elijah, Jacob, Jedidiah, Noah and Daniel, Aunt Katie and Uncle Samuel's sons, were playing baseball. Isaac, another son, stood near the house talking with Ellen Mast, the girl who'd loved him forever.

Ellen was a good friend, and Nell hoped that her cousin saw her in the right light—and soon. It was obvious to her that Isaac had similar feelings for Ellen but was, for some reason, holding back. She wondered if it had something to do with the trouble he'd gotten into two years back. Nell had never believed that Isaac had been responsible for the vandalism at Whittier's Store—none of them did. But Isaac had never defended himself or confessed the truth, and so he suffered because of it.

Her gaze followed the horses in the pasture.

The mares were running through the open space, beings of pure beauty in energy and form. Closer to the fence, goats munched contentedly on the grass. To the left were the Lapps' two Jersey milk cows.

She heard hens clucking from a pen near the barn. She smiled, wishing she'd brought Jonas. Naomi was too little to expose to curious eyes and small hands.

"Nell."

She stiffened. Why was she imagining his voice? It hurt that she was so caught up in her feelings for him that she pictured him everywhere.

"Nell, I have to talk with you." His touch on her arm convinced her that the voice was real.

She turned, locked gazes with him. There was a depth of emotion in his dark eyes that quickly vanished as they stared at one another.

A quick study of him revealed that he'd changed clothes. Gone were the Amish garments he'd worn yesterday. Today he was back to wearing jeans and a blue button-down, short-sleeved shirt.

"What are you doing here?" she demanded, all thoughts of her desire to talk with him gone in the reality of his presence.

"I was on my way home, but I wanted to talk with you first."

"Why?"

"To explain about my family."

"What?" She bit her lip and blinked rapidly. Why did being near him upset her so much? "I know about your family. Your sister told me."

"I'd like to tell you why I kept the Pierce name." He leaned against the fence rail beside her, his tall form seeming bigger and more present than ever before.

"James." She gestured to the gathering in the yard behind them.

He didn't seem to care that someone might be watching, listening. "My mother was raised in an Amish household. When she met and fell in love with my father, John Pierce, she made the choice to leave her community and marry him. They moved to Ohio where my dad set up his veterinary practice. They were happy. I was born a year and a half later, and years later, my sister Maggie was born."

"Maggie Troyer."

"Except she was Maggie Pierce. Then Abigail came into our lives. When she was just a small child, my father died when he was on a vet call. He'd had a massive heart attack. He was forty."

"I'm sorry." She gazed at him with sympathy. She could see that the loss still deeply affected him after all these years. "How old were you?"

"Thirteen."

"A time when a boy needs his father."

"During the weekend, I used to accompany him on calls. I was sick that Saturday and couldn't go. I had a cold. He told me to stay home." He paused, closed his eyes then opened them. "I should have gone. I might have been able to do something."

"Nay!" Nell cried. "What could you have done?"

"Called the ambulance. Something."

She drew a deep breath as she fought the urge to pull him into her arms and offer comfort. "Didn't someone call the ambulance?"

"The homeowner. But Dad was in the barn tending to a cow when he keeled over. By the time the man found him, it was too late."

"I'm so sorry," she said softly, reaching to touch his arm. "That must have been difficult." She no longer cared that they were standing in full view of everyone near the fence. Her concern was only for James. "Then your *mam* came home to Pennsylvania with you, didn't she?"

"Yes, she was suffering, grieving. I didn't want to leave Ohio. It had been my home. My father was buried there. I'd gone to school there, and my friends were there, but I didn't say a word. Mom was hurting so badly. I understood her need to be with family. But to leave the English world to live with my Amish grandparents was more than I could handle. I was a sullen, angry teenager, and I didn't make things easy for anyone once we'd moved back. Suddenly, not only had I lost my dad but also my life and my identity."

Nell studied him. He stared at the animals in the pasture, and she watched as, miraculously, a small smile came to his mouth.

"This view reminds me of one at my grandfather's. *Grossvadder* was a kind and patient man." He closed his eyes, shuddered. "I still miss him— both of them. My grandfather and grandmother."

He opened his eyes and fixed her with his dark gaze. "One day, I became so overwhelmed with grief that I broke down and cried. I sobbed as if I was a baby and I'd lost sight of my mother. *Grossvadder* saw me crying and nodded as if I had done the right thing to break down. He'd moved on without a word, but I could read his thoughts even as I cried. Afterward, we talked. He said it was good to be strong, but that it is a stronger man who allowed himself to cry and to heal. He taught me about God and love, and because of him, I learned to settle and enjoy my life at the farm until Adam's wife died. *Mam* took my sisters with her every day so that she could take care of Adam's two children while he grieved. Matthew was three and Rosie was a newborn. Adam's wife, Mary, died after giving birth to her."

Nell knew what it was like to lose someone you

loved. Lately she'd seemed to be moving past her grief until she mostly thought of Michael with simple affection. Only on occasion did the pain rear up and strike her when she least expected it.

"You didn't like your *mudder* helping Adam?"

James shook his head as he faced her and he met her gaze head-on. "I didn't mind that. I minded that she and Adam later fell in love and married. I felt as if their love was a betrayal to my father. It was wrong, but I was fifteen—what did I know about love? I'd had a girlfriend in high school—but it wasn't anything serious and our relationship didn't last. When Dad died, I made a vow to honor him by following in his footsteps. I would become a vet. I'd always thought I wanted to be one anyway, but my goal became more of an obsession after losing Dad."

He glanced back toward the yard and stared at her cousins playing baseball. His lips curved. "I used to play baseball in Little League and in school. I loved it."

He drew a sharp breath, then released it. "I attended public, not Amish, school. By the time we moved here, I was already finished with eighth grade. *Grossvadder* approved of me continuing at the closest high school. Mom understood. She had loved my father. I'd known that. I'd seen and felt their love. Mom knew that continuing my education was the only way I could become the vet I was determined to be."

"And you did," Nell said with warmth. She paused. "What happened after your *mudder* married Adam?"

"We moved to live with him, of course, and I became a nightmare. I acted terribly toward Adam. I was difficult, and I rebelled the only way I knew how by being cold, unfeeling and nasty to him."

Nell saw regret settle between his brows. This James she was learning about was even more appealing and more attractive to her. She bucked herself up with the reminder that the most they could ever be was friends—and that it would be wiser for her to keep her distance from him.

"I take it things eventually changed between you and Adam."

James flashed her a grin. "No thanks to me. I give Adam all the credit. The only time I ever behaved was at school. I studied hard because I was determined to get into a good college."

Nell was curious. "How did Adam change your relationship?"

"One day he'd had enough. It was late during my sophomore year. He took me aside, and we had a talk. Well, he talked, and I listened. He told me that he loved my mother and my sisters and that he loved me no matter how difficult I acted toward him. That his love won't stop because I wanted it to. He said that he wouldn't replace my dad and that he didn't want to. A dad's place in a son's life is important. He simply wanted to be my friend and to be there whenever I needed him."

"Oh, James… Adam is a *gut* man."

James blinked, his eyes suspiciously moist. "Yes, he is. He then told me that I needed to be a man, not a boy."

Nell raised her eyebrows, hurting for the boy he'd been and the man he was. "I doubted that went over well."

"Actually, it did. I understood what he was saying. I realized that God had given me Adam after He'd taken my father."

"James…"

"I'm not angry with God, Nell, but I do think that He took Dad home for reasons of His own."

"Matthew and Rosie might believe it's because they needed a *mudder*—your *mam*."

He smiled. "She loves them like her own." He slipped his hands into his front jeans pockets. Suddenly, he seemed uncomfortable as if he might have revealed too much of himself. "Adam became a father to me, and I let him. He's never been anything but fair and understanding, even when I chose to leave the community to attend Ohio State, my father's alma mater. And later when I left for Penn Vet—the University of Pennsylvania's Veterinary School. Even when I stayed in the Philadelphia area afterward and worked for six years in an animal hospital there."

"But then you decided to move back to Lancaster County."

"To be closer to my family," James said. "I realized that I was working all the time. I wasn't really living. My father would have hated that. He loved being a vet, but he loved his family more." He removed a hand from his pocket to run fingers through his dark hair. "I missed *Mam*, *Dat*, Maggie, Abby, Matt and Rosie."

She held back a smile as she noted how he'd slipped into his former Amish life pattern with the Pennsylvania Deitsch names for his mother and father.

"So now you know."

Nell didn't know how to respond. Why had she chosen to believe ill of this wonderful, kind man? Because she didn't want to have these warm and affectionate feelings for him.

"I should go," he said as he straightened away from the fence and faced the yard. "Work tomorrow." His brow furrowed. "I'll miss you, Nell. You were the best assistant a man could have."

Emotion rose as a knot in her throat. "I'm sure Janie is better," she said hoarsely.

"I doubt it." He looked up and apparently saw something that made him separate himself from her not only emotionally but physically, too. He drew back a few feet from her. "Matt," he greeted.

Nell smiled at James's brother. "*Hallo*, Matt. Tired of playing baseball?"

"*Nay.*" He glanced from her to James and back. "Did you like working for my *bruder*?"

"*Ja,*" Nell said, "I learned a lot from him. You know how I love caring for animals."

"I do." Matthew's expression had turned soft.

"I need to go," James said.

"I'll walk you to your car," Matthew offered.

"You just want to take another close look."

Matthew laughed. "Maybe."

James turned to Nell. "Goodbye, Nell. Thanks again for filling in at the clinic when I needed you."

"Thank you for Naomi and taking care of Jonas when he needed you."

"You're *willkomm*." James gave her a sad smile.

Then Nell watched him walk away, and her heart ached for what she couldn't have and what her life would never be.

Chapter Thirteen

It was late. Darkness had settled over the land. Nell had brought in the horses when she heard a car rumble down the driveway. James. He came to mind immediately. She closed the back barn door and hurried through the building to meet him out front. But it wasn't James who was getting out of his car. It was their *English* neighbor, Rick Martin.

"Nell," he said soberly when he caught sight of her. "I have bad news. Catherine Fisher was rushed to the hospital a few minutes ago."

"Ach, nay!" she breathed. "And Bishop John?"

"He went with her to the hospital. I've brought their son, Nicholas. Catherine asked if you would watch him."

Nell swallowed. "She mentioned me?"

"Yes, by name." Rick opened the back door of the car. The little two-year-old lay on the backseat. Curled up in sleep, the boy looked like a little angel. "He doesn't know what happened. He was upstairs napping when Catherine collapsed."

"I'm sorry," she murmured. She reached inside the car and lifted baby Nick into her arms. He cuddled against her, and she sighed. "Thank you for bringing him, Rick."

"I'll find out how she is and let you know."

Nell nodded. "I'm going to bring him inside and put him to bed before he wakes up."

She turned toward the house with the bishop's son in her arms. She didn't wait for Rick to leave as she entered the house. As she headed toward the stairs, she met her mother.

"Nell."

"'Tis Nicholas Fisher, *Mam*." Nell shifted to bring the child closer. "Catherine is in the hospital. John went with her. Rick brought him. Before the ambulance took her away, Catherine asked that I watch him."

Her mother's expression softened as she studied the sleeping child in Nell's arms. "You'll put him in your room?"

"Ja," Nell said. She eyed the child in her arms with warmth. "I wonder why Catherine asked for me?"

"Everyone has seen how you are with their animals, Nell. If you have enough love and compassion for animals, imagine how much you have for a little boy?"

She widened her eyes. "You think that's why?"

"I do." *Mam* smiled. "You're a kind and loving woman, and everyone sees it."

Nell started up the stairs then stopped. *"Mam?"*

"Ja, Nell?"

"What if someone loves the wrong person? Someone who isn't right for her?"

Her mother looked at her with love and understanding. "Does this someone recognize that it's best to avoid the wrong man?"

She nodded.

"Then you have your answer, Nell. Although God the Father might not disagree. The Lord wishes us to love all men."

Her heart was heavy as Nell climbed the stairs with the small boy in her arms. She felt terrible for Catherine and John. She was worried about little Nick, who would awaken in the morning looking for his mother.

With Nicholas in one arm, she pulled back the top layers on her bed. She laid the boy gently on the mattress and covered him with the sheet and quilt. Then she pulled up the chair that she'd kept in the corner of her room and sat—and she watched him until exhausted, she climbed onto the double bed next to him. She offered up a silent prayer that Nicholas would have his mother and father home by tomorrow morning. With that good thought, Nell was able to close her eyes and sleep.

"Catherine Fisher died during the night," *Mam* told James and his siblings at breakfast on Sunday morning. "John was by her side."

"When did you hear this?" Adam asked.

"Just a few minutes ago. Nell's *mudder* stopped by. It seems that Catherine's last words were that Nell take care of their little son, Nicholas, while she was in the hospital. She didn't realize that she wouldn't be coming home again."

James's thoughts went immediately to Nell. "Where is Nicholas now?"

"He's still with Nell. John's still at the hospital, making the final arrangements for his wife."

"What's going to happen now?" Matthew reached for a muffin and put it on his plate.

"Nicholas no longer has his mother. John will need to marry again and quickly for the sake of his son."

"Who would want to marry a grieving widower with a young child?" James really wanted to know.

"Nell might," *Mam* said. "She's single and well past the age of marrying. It would be a *gut* arrangement for the both of them."

"Nay!" James exclaimed. When his mother

stared, he blushed and looked away. "It makes no sense for them to rush into marriage. I know too many people who married in haste and then suffered afterward."

"But these people you know—they weren't of the Amish faith, were they?"

James shook his head. "No. But why would that make a difference?"

"It's not unusual for a man to take a wife simply for the sake of his motherless child. The couple will find love and respect with the passage of time," Adam explained.

Feeling a hot burning in his gut at the thought of Nell marrying another man, James couldn't let it go. "And if John..."

"Bishop John," his mother said.

"And if the bishop doesn't accept his new wife as someone he could love? What will that mean for the woman?" For Nell, he thought.

Adam looked sorrowful. "Only the Lord knows the answer to that question, James."

James looked from his stepfather to his mother. "*Dat*, you didn't," he reminded. "It wasn't until you fell in love with *Mam* that you asked her to marry you."

"*Ja*, 'tis true. I couldn't at first. I was grieving too much, but then your mother entered my heart like sunshine on a dark, stormy day. It was then that I asked her to marry me. I'd had an inkling that she had similar feelings for me."

"How?" James asked. "How did you know her feelings?"

Adam gazed at his wife with soft eyes. "She told me."

"She *what*?" It was Matthew who had spoken.

Mam laughed. "Not in words, *soohn*," she assured Matt, "but in looks and my caring for you and your sister."

Matthew joined in her laughter. "It would be fine if you'd told him, *Mam*, right off."

"Right for you," James said with good humor. "I would have been a nightmare worse than I already was if you'd married right after Mary died."

"I would have been right with you," Matthew admitted with a grim smile.

"Is there anything we can do?" Maggie asked. She'd been listening quietly up until now. "Nell may need some of Nicholas's things. We could get them for her."

"I'll go with you," Abigail offered.

"James?" Rosie said. "You know Nell. Maybe she'd like you to bring her little Nick's things?"

He looked at his stepsister and sisters. "I don't know—"

"That's a fine idea, James. You have a car. You can drive over to the bishop's house and gather what Nell will need."

"I could get there faster," James agreed. "What if John isn't home? How will we get in?"

"The bishop doesn't lock his house," Maggie said. "He trusts that God will protect his family and his home."

James frowned as he stood. God hadn't kept the man's wife from death's door. Not that he thought less of God. Life and death were simply the way of a person's existence. "Rosie, it was your idea. Would you like to come with me?"

Rosie stood and carried her breakfast dishes to the sink. "*Mam—*"

"Go, *dochter*. James needs your help as much as Nell is going to need his."

Leah sneaked into Nell's room where Nell lay awake next to the bishop's sleeping child. She motioned for her sister to step outside.

Nell frowned as she stood in the hallway.

"Nell, Catherine is dead." Leah flashed a look of concern toward the boy in Nell's bed. "She died during the night. There was something wrong with her heart."

"John—"

"Is devastated. He'll not be thinking of his son at a time like this. It could be the reason why Catherine asked you to care for him…because she knew she wouldn't be coming back."

Nell's eyes filled with tears. "But why me?"

She drew a shuddering breath. "What am I going to tell that little boy? Nicholas, your *mam* is dead, but it's okay because she is with the Lord?" She lifted a hand to brush back an escaped tendril of soft brown hair. "He'll never understand that. He's too young to know about God and death… and losing his *mudder*."

"Get dressed," Leah said. "We need to figure out a way to get more of Nicholas's things."

"*Ja*, Rick only brought Nicholas. He had no clothes, no diapers." Nell grimaced with wry humor as she glanced toward her bed. "I'm going to need clean sheets, I think."

Leah chuckled. "A wet bed is the least of your worries." She moved into the room. "I'll sit with him. *Dat* wants to see you. He's waiting for you downstairs."

Nell raised her eyebrows. "What could he possibly want—" Her eyes widened. "*Nay*, surely he won't suggest that I step in and marry John?"

"Only one way to find out."

"Fine. Let me change clothes, and I'll go down to see what he has to say."

"Remain calm," her sister instructed. "Don't lose your temper. If you stay calm, you'll retain the upper hand."

Dressed and ready to face her father, Nell went downstairs, pleased that Nicholas continued to sleep for now.

Arlin Stoltzfus was at the kitchen table. Her sisters and mother were absent. Having no one in the room was a sure sign that her father had something serious to say to her.

"Dat?" She entered the room as if she wasn't concerned with what he might say. She poured herself a cup of tea and then held up the teakettle. "Would you like some?"

Her father shook his head. *"Nay,* I've had my morning coffee. Sit down, Nell."

Nell sat, pretending an indifference that she was far from feeling. "Doughnuts! I love doughnuts. And there are powdered and chocolate glazed. I'll have one of each!" She knew she was rambling, but she couldn't seem to stop herself.

"Nell."

"Ja, Dat?"

"We need to talk about Nicholas—and John."

"Nicholas is still sleeping, poor *boo.*" She took a small bite of her powdered doughnut, chewed and swallowed. "I imagine John is devastated over losing Catherine. And Nicholas—how is he going to react when he learns that his *mudder* isn't coming home to him?"

"Nicholas will be fine once he gets another *mudder.*"

Nell stared at him. "Another *mudder*? No one can replace his *mudder.*"

"He can, if you marry John."

"*Dat*, the man just lost his wife. The last thing he'll want is to marry me—a stranger. I'll be happy to care for Nicholas until he has his time to grieve, but to even suggest that he marry so quickly…"

"You *will* marry him."

"I—*what*?"

"This is your opportunity for marriage. John is a fine man. He'll make you a *gut* husband. Nicholas is a sweet little *boo* who needs a mother."

Nell gazed at her father in shock. "*Dat*, surely you don't believe that God wants me to be Nicholas's mother?"

"There are many young women within our community, *dochter*. If God didn't want this, then why did Catherine specifically ask for you?"

"*Dat*," she whispered. "*Nay*." But what if the Lord did want this for her? What if this was the answer to her prayers regarding her forbidden love of James? If she married John, then she would have to get on with her life without James. It was something to think about. "I'll consider it, *Dat*."

Her father looked pleased. "Do that, but do it quickly. John is a practical man. He will want to marry again soon for the sake of his *soohn*."

Nell opened her mouth to object. She didn't believe for one second that John would be in a hurry to marry. Not when he was still grieving over the loss of his beloved Catherine.

With Rosie's help, James entered John Fisher's house and found clothes, a blanket and a basket of clean cloth diapers for Nicholas. They left as quickly as they'd come, and James drove right to the Stoltzfus farm so that he could hand over the boy's belongings to Nell.

His heart was pounding hard as he drove up to the Arlin Stoltzfus residence. Rosie opened her car door first and reached into the back for the basket of diapers. James carried the rest of the items—the boy's nightgown, some socks, shoes, little shirt and pants—and cute little straw and black felt hats.

His sister waited for him to join her before they climbed the steps to the large white house. James glanced at his sister and nodded. Rosie raised her hand and rapped her closed fist on the doorframe.

The screen door opened immediately, and James found himself face to face with Nell's sister Leah. "I—we've—" he said, including his younger stepsister, "picked up a few of Nicholas's things from the house."

Leah glanced from him to his sister. Rosie held up the wicker basket. "I have clean diapers."

"I brought his blanket and his garments—and

his hats." James smiled as he studied the hats that lay on the pile of clothing in his arms.

"That was kind of you," Leah finally said. She opened the screen door and stepped aside. "Come in. Please."

James followed Rosie into the house.

"You must have gone early," Nell's sister said.

"As soon as we heard," he admitted.

"Let me get Nell. You may take a seat if you'd like. There are doughnuts on the table and fresh coffee on the stove."

"Thank you." James exchanged glances with Rosie, then together they set the items they carried close by and sat down.

Nell came into the room less than a minute later. "James! Rosie, Leah said you brought Nick's clothes."

James stood as she walked into the room. "Yes, we thought you could use them, considering what happened."

The young Amish woman's eyes filled with tears. "He's going to need them."

"*Mam* said that Catherine asked for you to take care of him."

"*Ja*, I was surprised. I didn't know Catherine that well." She bit her lip, looked away. "*Dat* believes God has a plan."

"What kind of plan?" James asked. He had

a bad feeling about Arlin's belief in a plan that somehow involved Nell with the bishop's son.

Nell shook her head. "It doesn't matter."

"Nell," he began. "Can I do anything for you? Something? *Please*, I want to help."

He saw her swallow hard. "You've already done a lot by getting Nicholas's things for him," she said.

"Nell!" Leah called. "He's waking up!"

"I'm sorry," Nell whispered. "I have to go to him." Her gaze went to Rosie but settled longer on James. *"Danki."* She blinked back tears. It was as if she were saying goodbye. To him.

They didn't stay for doughnuts and coffee. James drove back to the house with his sister.

"What do you think Nell meant when she said that her *vadder* thinks that God has a plan?" Rosie asked, breaking the silence in the car.

"I don't know." But then he realized that he did. Arlin Stoltzfus had been wanting his daughter to marry, and with Catherine's death, Bishop John would be seeking a mother for his child.

No! James thought. He couldn't allow her to marry John Fisher. John would never love Nell like he did. But what could he do?

He was powerless to stop them from marrying. An *Englisher*, he had no right to marry Nell or to stop her from heeding her father's wishes.

Chapter Fourteen

Her *dat* was right. Bishop John was grieving but he would marry again for the sake of his young son. Nell herself was exhausted. She'd gotten little sleep since her *dat* had made the suggestion that she become John's new bride. And while it was true that she'd not found a man to marry on her own, Nell knew that she'd never find the love she'd once hoped to find in marriage. Not when she loved James, who could never be her husband.

Little Nicholas had taken to Nell as if she was the one who'd given him birth. Nell found out the reason why after learning just how ill Catherine had been since giving birth to her son. She'd been unable to take care of him except for short periods of time. Nicholas had spent time in several different neighboring households who cared for the little boy while Catherine had attempted to rest and recover. Only she never had.

The night she realized that she would soon become John Fisher's wife, Nell dreamed of Meg's hospital stay, of going for tea and hearing the beeping of life-support machines…and looking into a room and getting the shock of her life. Only it wasn't Michael in the room in her dream. The man in her dream was James, and when she saw him hooked up to machines, Nell cried out and fell to her knees. *"Nay! Nay!"* she screamed.

She woke, gasping for air, her heart pounding hard with the sudden concern that something had happened to her beloved James. She might not be able to have a life with him, but that didn't mean that she wouldn't think of him, worry about him, every single day for the rest of her life. Whether she was the bishop's wife or not.

Nell recalled little Nicholas and wondered if her screams had frightened him. She looked next to her to the empty space and remembered that Leah had taken him to sleep with her for the night. Nell had suffered from lack of sleep since learning of the child's mother's death. Leah had suggested that if Nicholas was with her, Nell might be able to rest without worry and with the possibility of sleeping late.

She rose and went downstairs. Her head hurt. Her heart ached. She didn't know how she was going to go through with the wedding. Because of Nicholas's age, *Dat* thought she and John should marry quickly. Nell wanted to wait until November, after the harvest, when it was wedding time.

"There is no reason to wait, Nell," her father had said time and again. "John's a widower. Widowers don't have to wait until the month of weddings."

"I want to wait," Nell insisted. "Unlike John, I have never been married. Don't I deserve a wedding like the other young women in our community."

"Nicholas needs you."

"I need the time. I'm happy to care for Nicholas before the wedding. There is no reason to wait for that."

And so her father had relented. Even John, Nell realized, seemed relieved. What kind of future would they have if both of them married only for the sake of a child?

An unhappy one, Nell thought, but then she didn't expect to be happy without James Pierce in her life.

The number of appointments had increased in Pierce Veterinary Clinic. James tried not to think of Nell's upcoming marriage to the bishop as he kept himself busy seeing patients during the week and worked hard in Adam's furniture store on Saturdays.

He was amazed at the change in his business.

He'd gone from worrying about his finances to raking in money. He should be glad. It was what he'd always wanted, but he realized that he was never going to feel successful. Because he was missing something—someone—vital in his life. *Nell.*

Two weeks had passed since he'd given her the child's belongings he'd retrieved from the bishop's house. He wondered if she was happy. Was she looking forward to her marriage? Did she love the thought of becoming Nicholas's mother for real?

He wondered how her dog, Jonas, was faring. If she had been one of his *English* clients, he would have called and found out if Jonas had suffered any ill effects from his bee sting. He could have stopped by the house and visited Naomi, seeing if there was anything Nell needed in the way of shots or food or cat toys.

"Last patient before the weekend, Dr. Pierce," Janie said as she entered the back room. "Exam room four."

"Thank you, Janie."

The last patient was a simple checkup with shots. He was tired when the day ended.

He came out to the front desk to hand Michelle the last patient's summary.

His receptionist eyed him intently. "Have you heard from Nell?"

He shook his head. "No. She's busy taking care of Nicholas Fisher. She's going to marry the boy's father."

"And you're going to just let her?"

"What else am I supposed to do? She belongs to the church. I'm considered an *Englisher*, and she can't marry me without serious consequences."

A small smile curved Michelle's lips. "So you've thought of marrying her," she said with satisfaction. "You love her." She shut down the computer and stood. "You should talk with her. Tell her how you feel."

He frowned. "You're awfully bossy lately." He sighed. "I appreciate the thought, but it won't help. I wouldn't hurt her with my love. If she marries me, she'll be shunned by her family and friends."

"If you were an *Englisher.*"

He stared at her, puzzled. "I am *English.*"

"But your family isn't."

"Yes, but…"

"Think about it, Dr. Pierce." She picked up her purse and went to the door. "I'm going home. I'll see you on Monday."

He couldn't help smiling at Michelle's attempts to throw him into Nell's path as he locked up and left. Even though there was no hope of that happening. Still, he drove out of the parking lot in the direction of the Stoltzfus residence. It wouldn't hurt to check on Jonas and Naomi… and to see Nell one last time before she became another man's wife.

"Hello! Is Nell home?"

Startled, Nell dropped a garment and spun. "James!"

"Nell, I didn't realize it was you. You look different with your kerchief." He smiled. "I hope you don't mind, but I stopped by to check on Jonas and Naomi."

"That's kind of you." She felt self-conscious in his presence. Wearing her work garments and taking down clothes didn't make her feel any less conspicuous and dowdy.

"Come and I'll show you where I keep them." She waved to her sister Ellie who was leaving the barn. Nell approached her, aware that James followed. "Ellie, would you please finish taking down the clothes?"

Ellie glanced from Nell to James and back. "*Ja*, I'll be happy to." She smiled. "Come to see her animals, I take it."

"I haven't seen Jonas since his bee sting, and Nell hasn't brought Naomi into the office yet."

Ellie met Nell's gaze. "I didn't feed either one. Wasn't sure if you wanted me to."

"That's fine, Ellie," Nell said. "I'll feed them. *Danki*."

She was overly conscious of the man beside her as they walked into the barn. "I did what I could to make them comfortable."

"Stop fretting, Nell. You love them. I know they're well cared for."

She stopped, looked at him and was shocked to see sincerity in his dark gaze…a small upward curve to his masculine mouth.

Nell heard Jonas's excitement as they drew close to his stall. He always seemed to know when she came to visit him. He'd bark and whimper and rise up on his hind legs as soon as he saw her.

"Jonas!" she crooned as she opened the stall door and went in. James followed behind her. "Guess who's here, buddy? 'Tis James."

"Hey, Jonas," he said softly. "May I examine you?" He bent and sat on the straw.

To Nell's delight, Jonas immediately crawled to James. He curled onto James's lap and looked up at him with big brown eyes. "How's your nose?" James bent and examined the injured area. "It looks good. All healed, huh?"

"*Ja*. He's suffered no ill aftereffects."

"Good." James smiled. "I brought you an EpiPen to keep on hand in case it ever happens again. I know Jonas wasn't allergic, but that could change if he gets stung again. Also, if he ever gets stung in his mouth, don't wait, Nell. Bring him in immediately. Okay?"

"I will," she promised, frightened by the thought. "I've kept him away from our flower beds."

James looked approving. "Unfortunately, you can't always avoid bee stings. Sometimes bees show up when you least expect them. Oh, and, Nell?"

She met his gaze. *"Ja?"*

"The same goes for hornets or wasps. Hornets and wasps will keep stinging. A bee loses its stinger, but they don't."

"I've never been stung," she admitted.

"I have, and it hurts terribly. Putting vinegar on it was the right thing to do. Remember that remedy if it happens to you or to Nicholas."

Tension rose between them at the mention of Nicholas.

Nell's kitten, Naomi, woke up and clambered over to James's side, easing the strain of the moment. She tried to crawl onto his lap beside Jonas. Nell saw that James looked surprised when Jonas allowed it. He shifted a tiny bit so that the kitten could snuggle against both of them.

Drawn to be included, Nell sat next to James. She could feel the heat of his skin when his hand accidentally brushed her as he moved Naomi into a different position.

"I'll take her," Nell said.

He handed her the kitten, his eyes never leaving hers. She experienced a flutter in her chest as she carefully took Naomi and held the cat to her cheek. "I love how she purrs."

"Like a motorboat," James agreed. "A soft one."

James gazed at the woman before him and experienced a painful lurch in his chest. He cared so much for her that it was a physical ache in his gut. The thought of her married to another man agonized him.

He realized that he should leave, but still he lingered. He shifted Jonas a little and reached for his medical bag. He quickly found what he was searching for and handed it to her.

"The EpiPen."

Nell looked at the pen, then accepted it. "How would I use it?"

He showed her how it worked. Then he placed Jonas carefully in his bed and stroked him one last time before he pushed to his feet. "I should go."

He had plans to be with family again this weekend. Nell surely had plans with the bishop and his son.

She set Naomi down and started to rise. James held out his hand and after a brief hesitation, she accepted his help. He released her hand as soon as she stood. He stepped back.

"Remember you don't need to call first if either of them is having an issue."

She murmured her agreement, and he followed her as she led the way out.

Emotion got ahold of him, and he stopped. "Nell."

She halted and turned. *"Ja?"*

"I—I care about you." He tried to gauge her reaction. "A lot." He heard her intake of breath, the way she released it shakily. "I know that you're going to marry the bishop, but—"

"James—"

"I know."

She seemed to struggle with her thoughts. "I care for you, too. But you know it won't work. I'm a member of the Amish church. I joined years ago. I can't leave, or I'll lose my family."

"I know," he whispered. "I won't say any more. I won't tell you how I wish you were mine."

"'Tis better this way. With you, I'd be shunned."

He felt a sharp pain. "I know. I'd never want that for you." He stiffened his spine, lifted his head and managed a smile. "I should go."

She nodded, turned, and continued on. James gazed at her nape beneath her kerchief and the back of her pretty spring green dress and tried not to feel devastated. Why did he have to fall in love with someone he couldn't have?

Always polite, Nell walked him to his car, and waited while he got in and turned the engine.

"Take care, Nell. Please don't let what I said stop you from seeking my veterinary services. I just had to say it one time. I won't make you uncomfortable again."

"Goodbye, James."

"Have a happy marriage, Nell."

He shifted into Reverse, backed up a few feet and made the turn toward the road. He pulled onto the pavement and saw the car too late to avoid it. The impact jerked him forward painfully, then forcefully bounced him back against the seat. And then he felt nothing.

Chapter Fifteen

Nell watched James drive away with a sinking heart. She knew he was upset. She would be marrying John, and there was nothing either of them could do but accept it.

She saw the flash of his car's right blinker, watched as his dark head swiveled as he checked both ways before he pulled out onto the road. She turned away, unable to watch the final moments of his departure. Then she heard a high-pitched squeal of tires, followed by a loud crash.

Nell took off running. There was the sound of a skid, then she saw the blur of a white vehicle as it whizzed past. Gasping, she reached the street and saw James slumped over the steering wheel of his Lexus.

As she ran forward, she glimpsed the pushed-in left front of his car, the tangle of broken fiberglass, metal and glass. She realized that James was sandwiched between his seat and the air bag. And she screamed.

"James!" Frantic, she ran to his driver's side. "James! James!"

"I'm all right," he muttered.

"*Nay*, don't move! You'll hurt yourself!"

"Nell! We thought we'd heard something!" Leah and her other sisters rushed to help.

"We need someone to call 911! We need to call 911!" Nell was beside herself as hysteria threatened to overwhelm. "How do we get to a phone?" The closest phone booth was down the road. "James needs help now! What do we do? What can *I* do?"

"I have a cell phone," Ellie said, pulling it from beneath her apron.

Nell stared, hoping she wasn't imagining things. "You have a cell phone?"

"What?" Ellie said defensively. "I clean for *English* families. They have to be able to reach me. The bishop approved it." She tugged on a pocket sewn to the underside of her apron.

"Thanks be to *Gott!*" Nell exclaimed. She didn't care that the phone and Ellie's pocket were deviations from the *Ordnung*. Pockets were fancy, but Nell didn't care. She was too happy, so very happy that her sister possessed both.

"Please, Ellie," she whispered. "Call 911." Close to James's window, she leaned in, mindful of the glass. "We've called for help."

James was barely able to nod. The air bag had deflated and finally she could see him. "Nell," he murmured.

"Don't talk. Don't move! Please, James!" She sounded high-strung, but she didn't care. This was James, the man she loved. Her recent nightmare about him in a hospital room came back to taunt and scare her.

Please let him be all right, she prayed. *Please, Lord. He's a* gut *man. Please help him. Please help me.*

It wasn't long before the ambulance arrived along with a local police officer. The EMT examined James, and as a precaution, the man used a brace to secure James's neck. Nell had to stifle a cry at the sight of it. She didn't want to upset James, who already had suffered enough.

The men carefully extracted him from the vehicle. They placed James gently on a stretcher, watchful of his condition and any unknown injuries.

The officer questioned Nell. "Did you see what happened?"

"I didn't see the accident. I saw James look both ways before he pulled onto the road. I turned to go back inside when I heard the sound of the impact, then of another car speeding away."

"Sounds like a hit and run," the officer said.

"Is James all right?" Nell asked anxiously.

"They'll be transporting him to the hospital to make sure," the technician said. "Things could have been worse."

Ja, *he could have died*. Nell couldn't keep her gaze off James who lay on the stretcher, looking frightfully vulnerable. She addressed the EMT. "May I talk with him a moment before you take him?"

"Not for long. We need to transport him—and the sooner the better."

Nell flashed her sisters a look. "Go," Leah said. "You don't have much time."

She was trembling as she approached the stretcher. "James," she whispered. "Are you *oll recht*?"

"I'll be fine, Nell."

"Your nose is swollen. You're going to have two black eyes." But she still thought of him as the most handsome man she'd ever known.

"The air bag," he breathed with a weak smile. He closed his eyes and exhaled.

"May I call the hospital to see how you are doing?" she asked, feeling suddenly shy.

He opened his eyes and focused his dark gaze on her. "Yes, if you want to."

"Do you want me to tell your family?"

He gazed at her with pain-filled dark eyes. "Yes, please. They'll be worried when I don't show. I planned to spend the weekend with them again."

"I'll go to them as soon as you leave," she promised, glad that she could be of help. "What about Michelle? Would you like me to call her, too?"

"No need. I'll give her a call if needed. I hope that I'll be examined and then released in a few hours."

Nell nodded, but she sincerely doubted that James would be staying anywhere but the hospital for a while.

"Time for him to go, miss," the technician said.

Nell stepped away, but she couldn't stop looking at him, caring…loving him. She shed silent tears. It didn't matter if she shouldn't care or love him. The only thing that mattered—and hurt—was that when he was well again, she would no longer have an excuse to see or talk with him. Her tears fell harder.

Her sisters joined her, standing around to offer her comfort as Nell watched the ambulance workers pick up James's stretcher and load it into the back of the vehicle.

Nell wiped away her tears and hurried forward. She needed to see him one last time. "James!"

"Nell." He gave her a genuine smile. "Don't worry."

She swallowed hard as she fought unsuccessfully to stop crying.

"Nell," he groaned.

She blinked, managed a grin. "I will talk with you soon."

And then they took him away. Nell stood a moment and as the ambulance drove away, her tears fell, streaking silently down her cheeks.

Leah slipped an arm around her waist. Ellie hugged her shoulders. Charlie stared a moment at the disappearing vehicle before she turned to Nell. "Let's get going. You need to tell the Troyers what happened."

Nell strove for control, drew herself up. "Will you take care of Nicholas for me?" she asked Leah. She heard a sound behind her and saw that Meg had readied the carriage.

"We'll go with you. I'll tell *Mam*. She'll be happy to watch him."

"All of you want to go?"

"I'm happy to watch Nick, but what will the Troyers think if all five of you drop in to give them the news?" *Mam* said, coming up from behind.

Blushing, concerned with how things might look to her parents, Nell said, "It might cause them more worry."

"Leah, Ellie, you go with Nell," *Dat* said. "Meg, you can help with Nicholas. Charlie, you can help your *mudder* with supper." His gaze was shrewd as he studied Nell. "He will be fine, Nell, but we will pray for him."

"Danki, Dat."

Within minutes, Nell and Ellie were in the family buggy as Leah drove at kicked-up speed toward the Troyers'.

Nell was still shaking. She stared ahead with her hands clenched in her lap. All three sisters were in the front seat. Ellie placed her hand over Nell's.

Nell blinked and turned her hand to squeeze Ellie's. "I'm glad you're coming," she admitted.

"We're sisters, and we are always here for you."

Nell thought that she might need her sisters more than ever in the coming weeks and months. During James's recovery. During her marriage—if she could go through with it—to John Fisher.

"Nell!" Matthew Troyer greeted them as they pulled into the yard.

Nell climbed down from the buggy with her sisters following. "Are your *eldres* home?"

He nodded. "What's wrong? Has something happened?"

"I'd like to tell all of you," she said quietly, but then she relented. "James was in an automobile accident." Her voice broke on the last word.

His face blanched. "Come inside."

They hurried toward the house while Nell's sisters waited outside.

"Mam! Dat!" he called as they entered the main hall.

"In the kitchen, Matthew!" his mother responded.

They entered the room to find the family getting ready to sit down to supper.

"Nell," Ruth greeted warmly.

Nell was unable to manage a smile. "I'm afraid that I have serious news. James was in an automobile accident this evening. He's in the hospital. He spoke with me before the ambulance took him. I think he'll be all right."

"Nay," his mother whispered as she rose, swaying. Adam immediately got up and put his arm around her.

Nell heard his sisters cry out, and she felt for them. She loved James, too, and knew it hurt to hear such terrible news.

A knock on the back door heralded her sister Ellie. Matthew opened it and invited her in. "I called Rick Martin," she said with the cell phone still in her hands. "He's on his way. He'll take you to the hospital."

"Danki," Ruth and Adam said at the same time.

The whole family was obviously devastated by the news.

"What happened?" Adam asked.

Nell explained that James had stopped in to check on Jonas and Naomi. "He told me before he left that he planned to spend the weekend with you."

"Ja," Matthew said. "He likes to visit on week-

ends and help with the farm work." He blinked rapidly, then drew himself up. "We like having him."

"We just got him back," his sister Maggie cried. "We can't lose him now."

Nell inhaled sharply. She didn't want to think about James dying, she didn't want to think about anything except for him to be walking through that door and awarding her his wonderful smile.

Impulsively, Nell reached out and gently squeezed his sister Maggie's hand.

Rick Martin arrived, and Nell watched as the Troyers piled into the car and left.

Nell returned to the buggy with her sisters. Ellie and Leah gave her a hug.

"He'll be *oll recht*," Ellie said.

"I hope so." Nell climbed into the buggy. She closed her eyes and offered up another silent prayer. *Please, Lord, allow James to heal. Please let him be well.*

At home, Nell and her sisters got out of the carriage and went into the house.

"How are the Troyers?" *Mam* asked as they came inside.

"Understandably upset," Leah said.

Nell wasn't hungry, but she knew her parents would worry if she didn't eat.

"Dinner is ready," Meg declared.

Nell sat at the table with her family, but the sick feeling in her stomach made it difficult to eat.

James had a doozy of a headache. His nose hurt, and his face, shoulders and chest felt like they had been beaten with a piece of wood. But all in all, considering what could have happened, James felt fortunate. He was alive and eventually would heal. Unless there was some injury the doctors hadn't discovered yet. Soon he would know.

He thought back to the moment of impact. A white sedan had been speeding in the opposite direction when James had made the right turn. For some reason he couldn't begin to fathom, the car crossed into his side of the road, only pulling back at the last second, crashing into the driver's side of his Lexus. If it wasn't for the air bag deployment, he figured he'd have been hurt a lot worse.

What had shocked him, however, was that the driver of the car had taken off. He'd been stunned and unaware of himself for a moment, but that lasted only several seconds. The next thing he heard was Nell's scream.

"Mr. Pierce," a nurse said as she entered his emergency room cubicle. "Your family is here."

"Are they allowed back?"

"Not all at the same time. Who would you like to see first?"

He immediately thought of Nell, but of course she wouldn't be with them. Would she?

"I'd like to see Adam please. Adam Troyer, my father."

The nurse left and moments later returned with Adam.

Adam came to the side of the bed, his expression worried, his brow creased with concern. "James, *soohn*, are you *oll recht*?"

"I'll live. I'm waiting for them to take me to X-ray." He managed a smile for the man who'd had nothing but love and patience for an angry teenager. "Is *Mam* ok?"

"She's worried as we all are. She'll come in next." He gazed at James, no doubt noting his swollen face, cut forehead and bruised nose and black eyes. "When your *mudder* sees you…" Adam began.

"*Ja*, I know." James shifted slightly and grimaced. "I needed to see you first so that you can prepare her."

"I will. I'm glad to see you awake and talking. We imagined the worst when we heard the news from Nell."

"Is she all right?" James asked quickly.

"Shaken up, but she gave us the message. Tried to ease our fears, but that's hard to do when you envision your *soohn* in a car crash, hurt, unconscious. Bleeding."

"I'm sorry, *Dat.*"

Adam waved his apology aside. "You did nothing wrong." He paused. "Nell…she must care for you a great deal."

"She does?" James asked with hope. But his hope died a quick death. Nell was going to marry the bishop.

"How do you feel about her?" Adam asked.

"I…" He looked away, stared at the curtain surrounding his hospital bed.

"You love her."

"Which is why I should stay away from her. Nell is a member of the church. There can be no future together for us." Although he'd like nothing more.

"What makes you think you can't have a future with her? You have the power to change your situation. Nell doesn't. You could come home, join the church and marry Nell."

For a moment, an idea that Michelle had given him appealed. "I can't." He sighed. "I spent all of my dad's money to become a veterinarian. I wanted to follow in his footsteps."

Adam pulled a chair closer to the bed and sat down. "And you went to school, worked hard, became a veterinarian and from what I hear from others, you are a *gut* one."

"Business is picking up."

"But why does having one thing negate having another? Members of our Amish community need basic veterinary care for their animals. It would be a simpler life, 'tis true. You wouldn't have your fancy car."

"The totaled car?" James commented with amusement.

Adam's lips twitched. "*Ja.* But James, I may be wrong, but you seem happier and more at peace when you stay at the farm. 'Tis almost as if you've missed the life."

James didn't say anything as thoughts ran through his mind. "I am happier there." He grew silent as realization dawned. "I do miss it."

"So? Why can't you return to the Amish life and still be a veterinarian? You'd be more of a country vet than a city one. It would be different, but it would be just as rewarding."

"It's something to think about," James agreed. Life in the Amish community with Nell as his wife? It sounded like the closest to heaven that a man could ever come to. If he still had a chance and Nell chose not to marry John.

Adam stood. "Your mother will be fretting. I'm going to leave and tell her to come in."

"*Danki, Dat.*"

Adam placed a gentle hand on his shoulder. "We can talk later."

"You won't tell *Mam*? Or anyone about my feelings for Nell?"

"For now. But if I were you, I'd talk about them with your *mudder*. She loves you and can offer a woman's side of things."

James nodded. He watched the curtain close behind Adam. Moments later, it opened again, and his mother walked in.

Nell didn't feel well. The food she ate settled like a lump in her belly. She knew she wasn't good company and that she should be spending more time with Nicholas. While her family moved to the great room after cleaning up after supper, Nell put Nicholas to bed, then went to sit on the front porch. The day lengthened, and darkness fell.

Was James all right? How was his family? The worry about James consumed her to the point where she felt physically ill. She loved him. He was an *Englisher*, and she had no right. He had obviously made the choice to leave the community and she couldn't ask him to change. She thought he had some affection for her. But love? His loving her would only complicate matters.

Nell heard the sound of a buggy—the clip-clop of a horse and the noise of metal wheels rolling over gravel before she saw the lights of the vehicle. As the carriage drew closer and stopped, she saw a flashlight flare, and someone stepped out, illuminated by the golden glow. It was James's sister Maggie. She realized that James's family was in the buggy behind her.

Nell felt instant alarm. "Is James *oll recht*?"

Maggie smiled. "He'll be fine, Nell." She approached and placed her hand on Nell's arm. "*Danki* for all you did for him."

Nell exhaled with relief. "Is he home?"

"*Nay.* He's still in the hospital. They want to keep him overnight and maybe one more day. He's battered and bruised, and he broke his collarbone. He won't be working at the clinic for a while, I'm afraid."

"*Ach, nay!*" Nell couldn't imagine James not working at the clinic for any length of time. Recalling how much being a veterinarian meant to him, she knew it would upset him to stay away.

"*Danki* for stopping by and telling me." It was late. His family didn't have to go to the trouble of letting her know, but she greatly appreciated it. She wondered if she would have been able to sleep if she didn't.

"We didn't just stop for that," James's sister said. "James wants you to use this until he gets out of the hospital."

It was his cell phone. Maggie extended it toward her, and Nell accepted it, her mind reeling from his thoughtful concern for her.

Maggie smiled. "He'll call you. Said he wants to talk with you himself."

She swallowed hard. "That's kind of him."

The other young woman nodded. "I should go."

Nell walked her to the buggy and the rest of the family who had remained inside. "I'm glad that James will be *oll recht*," she told them.

"We are, too," his *mam* said, echoed by Adam and his other siblings.

"*Danki* for what you did," Matthew said quietly.

"I did what I needed—wanted—to do. No thanks necessary."

Once Maggie was settled in the vehicle, Nell stepped back, clutching James's cell phone against her.

"Nell!" Maggie called as the buggy moved. "James said you can charge the phone at the clinic."

Nell hadn't thought about the phone battery dying. What if there wasn't enough charge left to answer James's phone call?

The Troyer family left, and Nell went back to the house. She entered the great room. "I think I'll head up to bed. Nicholas hasn't woken up, has he?"

"*Nay*," her mother said. "He's sleeping soundly." She smiled. "*Gut* night, Nell."

Her siblings echoed her mother's good-night. Her father eyed her carefully. If he noticed the cell phone in her hands, he didn't comment. "Sleep well, *dochter*. You did well today."

Blinking back tears, Nell murmured good-night, then quickly spun and headed toward the stairs. James's phone felt warm to the touch. It felt like she was holding his hand. She sighed, feeling close to him. She couldn't believe he'd sent her his cell phone.

After reaching the top landing, Nell walked the short distance down the hall to her bedroom. She looked inside, but didn't see Nicholas. She paused. Did Leah put him in her bed again?

She checked and found him sound asleep just as her mother had said. She was surprised to see that someone had brought in a crib for him. Why they'd put it in with Leah, she had no idea. She would ask them in the morning, not tonight. Not when she was expecting James to call at some point.

She hit a button on the phone, saw the face light up and was relieved to discover that the phone was fully charged. She set it carefully on her night table. James would probably call her tomorrow. She could rest easy tonight at least. She looked forward to talking with him. Just to assure herself that he is all right, she thought.

A short while later, Nell fell asleep and slept through the night until the soft ringtone of the cell phone next to her bed woke her the next morning.

Chapter Sixteen

"James?"

"Yes, Nell."

Nell closed her eyes. The sound of his deep familiar voice moved her through an ever-changing realm of emotion. "How are you feeling?"

His slight chuckle quickly died. "Like I've been run over by a truck."

She inhaled sharply. "I'm sorry."

"What for?" His genuine puzzlement filtered through the phone connection. "You have nothing to be sorry about." He paused. "Thank you for coming to my rescue."

"I didn't do much."

"Nonsense. You did a lot. You got me help. Told my family. Cared."

Nell's heart started to thump hard. "I did what anyone would do." But it was more. She loved him, but she shouldn't. Still she couldn't hang up the phone.

A few seconds of silence. "Maggie said that you'll be staying another day in the hospital."

"Yes. Unless they decide to release me sooner. I have some bruising they are concerned about… and my head. I think once they see I'm all right, the doctor will allow me to leave."

Nell couldn't forget the awful image of him trapped in his car behind the airbag. Her mind switched to her awful dream, and she gave a little sob.

"Nell? What's wrong?"

"You were in a car accident."

"I know, sweetheart. Believe me, I know."

He said it with such dry humor that Nell couldn't help but laugh. She missed this man. How was she going to live without him? His endearment warmed her as much as it frightened her. She had to believe that it was his condition and pain medication.

"*Danki* for giving me the use of your cell phone. I was worried about you. 'Tis *gut* to hear your voice."

He didn't immediately reply, and a tense awareness sprang up between them. "I feel the same. It's good to hear your voice. It's not the same in the office without you." She heard him draw a breath. "I miss you."

"James—"

"Nell, it's okay. We're just talking."

He was right. "*Ja*, just talking," she agreed. "Maggie said you won't be able to work in the clinic for a while. What will you do?"

"I'm going to call an old college buddy of mine. We both attended Penn Vet, and we both took our first jobs at the same animal hospital after graduation. I left the practice, but he still works there. I'm hoping that he'll be able to get away for a time and fill in for me."

And if he doesn't, Nell wondered, *then what will you do?*

"If it doesn't work with Andrew—that's his name, Andrew Brighton. He's English." He chuckled. "To you, we're all English, but Drew is truly an Englishman. He's from Great Britain."

"He has an accent?" she asked, and her lips curved into a reluctant smile.

"You like men with accents?" He made a growl of displeasure. "Ignore me. I'm hurting, and it's almost time for my pain pill."

"I should let you go."

"Yeah. The nurse is here to take my vitals." A voice asked him something on the other end of the line, and Nell heard James mumble something in reply. She wished she could see him. It was reassuring to hear his voice, but she wanted to see him so she could gauge with her own eyes how he was faring.

"Nell, are you still there?"

"*Ja*, I'm still here."

"May I call you again?"

How could she say no? *"Ja."*

"I'll call you after lunch—about one?"

"I'll be here." She should remind him about Nicholas, that the little boy might need her, but she didn't.

"Have a good morning, Nell."

"Feel better, James."

"I already am…after talking with you."

And with that, he hung up.

Nell stared at the phone, wondering what she was doing—what they were doing. She was going to marry the bishop! She shouldn't be talking with James. It was wrong. Just as wrong as it was to love James.

She tried but couldn't convince herself to return James's phone to Maggie. No, she needed—enjoyed—talking with him too much.

One o'clock came and went, and Nell grew worried. What if James's condition had taken a turn for the worse?

She started to panic. She flipped open the phone, pressed some buttons. She read the word *Recents* on the screen. She saw the time next to the number. Was that his hospital room telephone number?

She was behind the barn in the pasture. Leah was in the house with Nicholas. *Mam* and her other sisters had gone into town. Her father was at Aunt Katie's with Uncle Samuel. He had said he wanted to ask her uncle about adding on to the house.

Dare she call that number? She was concerned. If he didn't call soon, she would call the hospital...

The phone vibrated in her hands as she heard the familiar ringtone. She didn't know what the tune was. The only music the *Ordnung* permitted was the hymns from the *Ausbund* that they sang during church services.

The music continued, and Nell broke away from her thoughts to answer.

"Nell? Are you there?"

"*Ja*, James. Are you *oll recht*? I was worried."

"I'm sorry. I know it's later than one, but the doctor was in my room, and I couldn't call."

She experienced a knot in her belly. She had a mental image of him in bed, ill, sore, hurting. She closed her eyes, tightened her grip on the cell phone.

"What did the doctor say?"

"That I'm doing well. I'm being released this afternoon."

"You're going home?"

"Not to my apartment. I live over Mattie Mast's Bakery. The doctor wants me to avoid stairs."

Where would he stay? "You'll be staying with your family," she guessed. It made sense. He'd be comfortable, cared for, and he already enjoyed his weekends there.

"Yes, I'll stay with my mother and Adam. I've called Rick Martin. He's going to come for me when the paperwork for my release is ready."

She heard movement as if he were shifting the phone. "Will you come see me?" he asked.

Dare she?

"You can bring me back my cell phone."

"When?" she asked as she felt her face heat. Fortunately, he couldn't read her thoughts or see her blush.

"I'll borrow Rick's cell to call you once I get to the farmhouse."

Silence reigned between them for several seconds, which seemed longer. "Nell? Will you come?"

"*Ja*, I'll come." She could sense his relief that she would be visiting. "I know that you're eager to get your phone back."

"No, Nell. I'm eager to see you."

"The nurse will go over your instructions, then you'll be able to leave," Dr. Mark Keller said.

"Thanks, Doc."

The man smiled. "I'm glad it was nothing serious, James. It does upset me to think that I'll need to find another vet. I like you and so does Fifi." He grimaced as he said the name. "Frankly, I'm not particularly happy with my wife's name choice for our miniature French poodle."

James grinned. "Maybe you can tell her that it's too common for French poodles, that yours is special, and she needs to come up with a name that is unique."

Dressed in green scrubs after having been on call for most of the night, the man looked like the competent and confident surgeon and internist that he was. However, his expression lacked confidence as he talked about dealing with his wife about their dog. "Any suggestions?"

James gave it some thought. "None that immediately come to mind." He grinned. "Check the internet. Find some fancy French name."

The Kellers had come into his office a while ago with their miniature poodle that was just old enough to be taken from its mother. They had brought her to him straight from where they'd gotten her. This was their first puppy.

"The internet." The doctor laughed. "I'll do that."

James felt dizzy as he swung his legs off the side of the bed.

"Remember to take it easy. Don't go into the

office for any reason for at least two weeks." He paused. "You have a broken collarbone," he reminded him.

James sighed. "I know."

"It will be longer before you can see patients—about six weeks. What will you do?"

"I called a friend of mine to cover for me."

"Is he good?"

"Yes, he's good," James assured him. "We went to school together, worked in the same practice outside Philly."

The doctor looked relieved. "Maybe we'll get lucky and won't need a vet before your return to work." He looked over his shoulder at someone James couldn't see. "There is an officer here to speak with you. Says he found the hit-and-run driver."

James closed his eyes as another wave of dizziness swept over him. "Okay. Send him in."

"James—or should I say, Dr. Pierce?"

"James is fine." He managed a smile. "I'm your patient. You're not mine."

The doctor's mouth curved briefly in response. "Do you need another pain pill?"

"No, I already feel as weak as a baby lamb."

"Nevertheless, I'll send a prescription home with you. Given where you're going, I'll also have it filled in the hospital pharmacy. I'll ask the nurse to wait until it's filled before releasing you."

"Thanks." James stopped the doctor as he started to leave. "What about *Abella*?"

The man looked thoughtful, then his features brightened. "I like it. Now I just have to convince my wife."

Dr. Keller left, and the police officer entered the room. "Mr. Pierce," he greeted. "I'm Officer Todd Matheson. We found the person who hit you…"

James was told it was a teenager. A seventeen-year-old girl. James experienced a myriad of emotions as he listened to what Officer Matheson was telling him.

"She saw a rabbit on the road. She swerved to avoid hitting it."

James could understand the quick reflex that would have someone trying to preserve an animal's life. Who would understand better than he about valuing an animal?

"What will happen to her?" James asked. "You won't press charges, will you?"

"It's complicated. She did surrender herself at the station." James was surprised to see concern flicker across the officer's features. "I think there's more to it," the man said. "She was sobbing, crying hysterically, when she came in. She kept saying, 'Don't tell them. Please don't tell them.'"

"Who?" James asked.

"Apparently, she's in the foster care system. She didn't want her foster parents to know. It was almost as if she is terrified of them."

James frowned. "Does she have reason to be?"

"She was driving their car. Maybe she was afraid she'd get in trouble."

"Do you believe that?"

Officer Matheson shook his head. He looked quite intimidating in his police uniform, but there was something about him that told James the man was more compassionate and caring than most.

"Can you find out?" James hated the thought that a young girl had made one mistake that could make her life more miserable than it already was.

"I'm certainly going to try."

Later, as he sat buckled carefully into the passenger seat of Rick's car, James thought about the girl who had hit him and run. His mind naturally veered to Nell. What if it had been Nell who was the seventeen-year-old driver? Of course, she'd had a much better upbringing than Sophie Bennett apparently had. And she was Amish and would never get behind the wheel of a car. *Sophie.* That was the girl's name.

"You feeling all right?" Rick asked.

"Sorry. Preoccupied with what I learned today." He saw the man's curiosity and decided to satisfy it. Rick Martin had been a godsend to his family. Telling him about Sophie was the least he could do.

"The police found the hit-and-run driver." James went on to tell him about the girl, the officer's suspicions and James's own concern for a teenager he'd never met.

"I hope they go easy on her," Rick said. "Sounds like they might need to find her a safe home with loving foster parents who will take good care of her."

"Yeah." James couldn't agree more.

A few minutes later, Rick pulled the car into the Troyers' driveway and drove close to the house.

"Thanks, Rick." James reached gingerly into his front pocket, trying not to wince at the ensuing pain. He pulled out a few bills that he'd taken from his wallet earlier. He'd put his wallet in the bag with his medication and paperwork.

"No." Rick placed a hand on his arm to stop him. "No payment. I won't take it. You helped our guinea pig, Tilly. Our daughter was beside herself until you took a look at her." He continued, "You wouldn't let us pay. Said it was nothing. But it was something to Jill and to me. So, no, I will not take your money—ever."

"Rick—"

"Ever, Doc. Or you or your family won't get another ride from me."

James stared at him in shock. Then he saw the tiny grin that hovered over Rick's lips. "Oh, I get it." He smiled. "Thanks."

"You're welcome."

"Does this mean that I can borrow your cell phone if I need it?"

He handed James his phone. "What happened to yours?"

"A friend has it."

James quickly made the call, was glad when Nell picked up after the first ring. "I'm home," he said. "Just arrived."

"How are you feeling?" Nell asked with concern.

"Fine."

"When do you want me to visit?"

"Now?"

"I'll be there soon."

"Okay. I'll see you soon."

James ended the call and handed Rick back his phone, grateful when the man didn't ask him who he'd been calling. "Thanks."

"The phone call will cost you," the man joked.

James laughed. The door to the Troyer house opened, and every member of his family came hurrying to see him.

"Gang's all here."

"Nice gang," Rick commented.

James agreed. "Yes, the best."

The door opened, and Adam reached in to help him rise. His mother and sisters fussed over him while Matthew stayed behind a few moments, apparently to discuss something with Rick.

Once inside the house, with his mother on one side and his stepfather on the other, James was escorted to the great room where he was lowered into a comfortable easy chair.

"We've set up a bed in the sewing room for you. You'll have plenty of space. We didn't want you to go up and down the stairs. This way you'll be comfortable, and we'll be close if you need us."

"Danki, Mam. Dat." His gaze swept over his siblings, including Matthew who was carrying the plastic bag from the hospital. "All of you."

"You look pale," Maggie said. "Do you have your medicine?"

"It's in here," Matthew said as he approached and handed it to *Mam.*

His family all stood around him, making him feel slightly uncomfortable. He stared back at them. "What?" he finally asked.

"Your poor face."

"It's bad?"

"Could be worse," Matthew said.

They all laughed, and the tension that had crept into the room dispelled.

"Tea!" *Mam* exclaimed.

"Mam?" James called her back. "Make enough for one more?"

She gave him a curious look.

"Nell is coming. She likes tea, I think." He tried to keep his thoughts private and quickly said, "She's bringing back my cell phone."

Mam nodded, and she along with his sisters headed toward the kitchen while discussing what food they'd serve once Nell got there.

She came within the hour. James heard her voice as she entered through the kitchen. He suddenly felt like a nervous schoolboy. Ever since he'd talked about her with Adam, he couldn't get the possibility of her in his life out of his mind.

Dr. Drew Brighton would start on Monday. Much to James's delight, when he'd talked with his friend this morning, he'd learned that Drew was tired of his job at the animal hospital. He'd grown up in a rural area, and the city life was starting to get to him. "I'd love a chance to help you out," the man had said in his thick British accent.

And that got James to thinking. He wouldn't mention it to anyone. Not until he knew if it would work or not.

Nell walked into the room, stealing his attention immediately. She was a vision of loveliness in her purple dress and black apron and prayer *kapp*. He gazed at her as she approached, holding his cell phone. She seemed shy. He heard her inhale sharply as she drew near.

"James," she gasped, "your injuries!"

"I look like a bit of a monster, don't I?"

"*Nay*, not that." She took a chair next to his. His family, James noted, had thankfully made themselves scarce. "I'm sorry for your pain."

He regarded her with affection. "I'm fine."

"You don't look it!"

"You sound as if you care," he teased. He saw something in her expression that gave him pause.

"I care. We're friends, *ja*?" She stared at him, looked away. "Have you forgotten about John?"

"How could I forget?" he said. "Although I'd like nothing more."

Nell was more than a friend, and he figured she knew it. But for now, she believed that she would be marrying the bishop, unless he could figure out a way to convince her otherwise.

"*Mam's* making tea. Will you stay for a cup?" he asked.

She nodded and happened to glance down at the phone in her hands. "Here." She extended it to him. *"Danki."*

He accepted it and placed it on a nearby table. "You figured out how to work it easily enough." He should be thanking her for letting him call her. She could have refused the phone, and he would have had no way to talk with her. It was her voice that brightened his day, made the pain of his injuries more bearable. *Nell soothes me as she does the animals*. His lips twisted. What did that say about him?

"*Ja*, it took some learning, but it wasn't as hard as I thought. It's not what they call a smartphone, is it?"

He shook his head, unable to pull his gaze from her face. "No. It's just a flip phone. I don't like fancy technology. It's wasted on me." He loved the color of her hair...her warm brown eyes. The warmth of her smile when she was amused. The rich vibrancy of her laughter... He sighed, glanced away.

She chuckled. "Like your office computer." Her brow furrowed. "What's wrong?"

"Nothing. Everything's fine." He returned his focus to her with a smile, drinking in the sight of her as a thirsty man longs for a glass of cold water.

She stayed just long enough to finish her tea and have a piece of cake. It seemed like she'd just arrived when she stood and said she had to leave.

"Stop by again, Nell," Maggie invited.

His sister Abigail had collected the dishes and stood with a pile in her hands. "*Ja*, Nell, come see us." James's mother, Ruth, and sister Rosie echoed his other sisters' sentiment.

James watched Nell interact with his family.

They liked her, a genuine like and respect that told James that Nell could easily become a member of the family.

Nell turned her attention his way. "Take care of yourself, James," she said. "Feel better soon."

"Will you come see me?"

"I don't know." She blinked, looked away, then glanced back. "I will if I can."

The fact that he couldn't get her to agree worried him. What if he was wrong about Nell's feelings for him? What if she wanted to marry John and be a mother to his son, Nicholas? He watched helplessly as she paused in the archway as she was leaving and met his gaze.

And then he held on to hope. Joy filled his chest, stealing his breath as he saw a longing that mirrored his own. If he could have risen without aid, he would have gone to her. For now, he could only keep his feelings to himself and watch her leave, until he knew whether or not all would go according to plan.

Chapter Seventeen

James had called Michelle and Janie after he'd confirmed with Drew that his friend would cover for him while he was recuperating. Michelle had been extremely upset to learn about his accident. When she'd asked how it happened, he told her that someone hit him on the road near Arlin Stoltzfus's place.

"I'm glad Nell was there for you," she'd said softly.

Janie was more matter of fact about his injuries. "I'll help Dr. Brighton get situated in the office." Then she'd wished him a quick recovery.

Midmorning on Monday, James called the office to speak with Drew. "How are things going?" he asked.

"Fine. You've got a busy practice," Drew said. "I never imagined you were this successful."

"Ha! Didn't think I had it in me, huh?" James

couldn't bring himself to confess how hard things had been before they'd suddenly got better. "Does it bother you to be working in a successful practice?"

Drew snorted. "No, not at all. In fact, I'm enjoying myself." He hesitated. "Take all the time you need."

"I will." James had a sudden thought. "Drew, stop by the house on your way home tomorrow, will you?"

"Be happy to. Haven't seen you in a while. I'd like to get a glimpse of how ugly you've gotten with that banged-up face."

Drew had been staying at James's apartment since Sunday night. The arrangement worked well for both of them. It was nice to know that someone he trusted would be living in his apartment while he stayed with his mother and Adam.

"Funny," James said with a laugh.

As he closed his cell phone, he got more comfortable in the chair and shut his eyes. He must have dozed, because the next thing he know it was late afternoon.

He blinked and focused as someone came into the room.

"Gut, you're awake. You've skipped lunch. I'll make you a snack."

"Mam," he said as she turned to go back into the kitchen. "I've asked my friend Drew to stop by."

"The one who is running the practice while you're recovering?"

"Yes."

"Does he like tea or coffee?"

James chuckled. "The man's a Brit—from England. He's a tea man all the way."

His mother eyed him with amusement. "Will he be happy with zucchini cakes and lemon squares with his tea, or do I need to pull out my recipe for scones?"

"I'm sure whatever you have will be fine."

Just before suppertime, Drew appeared and stared down at him aghast. "You look like a Sasquatch attacked you, James."

"Sasquatch?"

"The huge, hairy caveman people say they've seen living in the woods. You look dreadful."

"Thanks, Drew. I appreciate the sentiment."

The British man grinned. "All right, that might have sounded a bit dramatic."

"You think?"

"But seriously, James, you look awful."

"So I'm told." He studied his old friend and realized that he missed Drew's dry sense of humor and quick wit. "I've got a proposition for you."

Drew folded his long body into a nearby chair. "Do tell."

And so James did.

Drew cocked his head as he listened. "Seriously?" he asked. "Wow, I never thought this of you."

"When you know, you know." James stared at him. "Do we have a deal?"

Drew smiled slowly and stuck out his hand. James grabbed it and they shook it twice, then again. "Deal."

James beamed, feeling hopeful for the first time in his life.

Nell steered her buggy into the clinic parking lot and to the back of the building. A black SUV was parked in James's spot. For a minute she stared, recalling the wonderful times she had working with James, learning about the man, falling in love with him.

But now it was over, and she'd never again have a reason to spend time with him. She would consent to marry John as soon as possible. She would only allow herself one more visit this afternoon to see how he was faring.

With a silent sob, she got out, hitched up her horse then circled the building to enter through the front door.

Michelle sat in her usual spot behind the desk. "Nell!" Her eyes widened with delight as Nell approached.

"Lunch?" Nell asked of the girl she'd gotten to

know since she'd first brought Jonas to the clinic. The two women had shared an instant connection.

"Definitely!" The other woman stood. "Janie just showed in the last patient. I'll tell Drew that I'm leaving and ask Janie to handle the last check-out."

Nell sat while Michelle went into the back room. The woman returned within minutes and smiled. "Last patient is almost done. Do you mind waiting?" She lowered her voice. "I'd rather check out the last one myself since it's so close."

"I'll be happy to wait."

Michelle grinned.

Nell picked up a dog magazine and leafed through it. She looked up when she heard voices and watched as a tall, handsome blond man in a lab coat escorted a woman with a cat carrier to the front desk. Nell felt a jolt. She recognized the cat owner.

"You have nothing to be alarmed about, Mrs. Rogan. Your kitten will be fine. I suggest you keep her away from Boots for a while…or at least Boots's food." The man was obviously British. His richly accented tone was pleasing to her ear. *James's friend Andrew Brighton.*

"I will," Edith Rogan promised. The older woman turned, saw her sitting in the waiting room. "Nell!" she greeted with obvious delight. "How are you?"

"I'm well, Mrs. Rogan."

"I miss seeing you in the office."

Nell smiled. "I enjoyed working here."

"Why are you here? Is something wrong with kitty?" Mrs. Rogan asked.

"Nope," Michelle piped up before Nell could answer. "She's my lunch date."

"Naomi is wonderful," Nell assured.

Mrs. Rogan looked pleased. "Enjoy your lunch, Nell. It was nice seeing you again."

"You, too, Mrs. Rogan."

Nell rose as the woman went to the door. Mrs. Rogan halted and turned. "I was sorry to learn what happened to Dr. Pierce."

"*Ja*, it was terrible."

"He doing all right?"

"He'll be fine. I thought I'd stop by and visit with him later today."

"You give him my regards."

"I will, Mrs. Rogan. Thank you."

"Aren't you going to introduce us?" a rich British voice asked.

Nell turned and met the man's curious gaze.

"This is Nell Stoltzfus," Michelle said. "Nell, Dr. Andrew Brighton."

"It's nice to meet you, Nell," he said with gray eyes that regarded her warmly.

She felt her face heat. "Nice to meet you, too."

Michelle watched the exchange with amusement. "We're going to go, Drew. I'll be back in an hour."

"Take as long as you like," Drew said, withdrawing his gaze from Nell.

"I'll take the rest of the day," Michelle teased.

"Better not," the man quipped. "It seems Nell here has plans for the afternoon."

Michelle grabbed her arm and escorted her to the front door. "Come on, Nell. Don't let this Brit embarrass you."

"Embarrass her!" he exclaimed. "That wasn't my intention!"

Michelle grinned as she shut the door, blocking out his words. "He is just too easy to tease!"

Nell laughed. "You are terrible."

"I know. Don't you love it!" She pulled Nell toward her car. "No offense, but I'm driving."

"Where are we going?"

"I know a little place," Michelle said.

Ten minutes later, they were seated in Katie's Kitchen in Ronks, sipping on fresh-brewed ice tea and enjoying their delicious yeast rolls with the restaurant's signature peanut butter spread. Nell had been there before and enjoyed their food.

"So you're going to see James today," Michelle said after the two had caught up on news of their families.

"*Ja.* I haven't seen him since the day after it happened."

"You visited him in the hospital."

Nell shook her head. "*Nay*. At his family farm where he's recovering." She took a sip of her ice tea. "Have you heard from him?"

Michelle finished chewing a bite of roll before answering. "Yesterday. He called to speak with Drew." She smiled. "He sounded good. Said he was feeling better."

"He was really hurt, Michelle. His face…" Nell blanched as she recalled the accident.

The other woman reached across the table to squeeze Nell's hand. "You were there. It must have been awful."

Nell released a sharp breath. "You have no idea." She shifted uncomfortably when Michelle's gaze sharpened.

"Dr. Brighton is working out?" Nell said, changing the subject.

"Oh, yes. He is wonderful. He's like James in many ways. Both are kind and compassionate men with a deep love for animals."

Nell smiled. "I'm glad James was able to call on someone to help so quickly."

"Yes. You won't believe how busy we've become!"

Nell was glad. She'd done all she could to help James build his practice, handing out his business cards, getting others to hand out cards and recommend the clinic…spreading the word throughout her Amish community.

All too soon, Michelle's lunch hour was up, and they were heading back to the clinic.

"We'll have to do this again," Michelle said with warmth as she pulled into the lot and parked. The women got out and met in front of the vehicle.

"*Ja*, I'd like that."

Michelle encircled her with her arms. "Great to see you. Take care of yourself."

"I will. You too."

Michelle went inside, and Nell suddenly experienced nervous excitement as she unhitched Daisy and climbed into her buggy. It was time to see James. She both yearned for and dreaded the visit.

Last time. Soon, James would be well and back to work, and except for the rare occasion when she might need to call on him for her animals' medical care, she wouldn't have much opportunity to see him.

Losing Michael had been devastating, because Michael had died while he'd been on his way to her. But losing James would be different. She was older now, and she'd had a chance to mourn Michael's death.

When she left James this afternoon, she knew

she would feel destroyed. She was glad that James would be out there in the world, doing what he loved to do. It was her only comfort. But him being so close yet out of reach was going to hurt her like nothing else ever had.

James was still sore but feeling better. He knew his face was black-and-blue. His sister had used his battered looks to coerce him into staying put in the chair. But he could no longer remain inactive. He knew he looked terrible, but thanks to ice and time to heal, the swelling around his nose had gone down. The ache in his muscles had become bearable with no need of medication to help him with the pain.

He knew he'd been given orders to rest for the next two weeks, but he was going crazy. Maybe if he just went outside for a little while. Surely, he could sit on the front porch and read or something. Anywhere but the inside of the house which he loved but had had enough of for now.

He stood and went into the kitchen. His mother and sister Abigail were at the table, snapping green beans they had picked from their vegetable garden.

"You should have called out if you needed something," *Mam* said.

"I had to move. Seems like I've been sitting in that chair for months."

His sister smirked. "James, 'tis only been five days."

He sighed. "I know. I'm not used to the inactivity. I want to be outside helping *Dat* and Matt."

"We can't allow you to do that."

The kitchen windows were open, and a light breeze blew into the house helping with the heat.

"'Tis a while before supper. Do you want something to eat?"

"If I eat any more, I'll gain ten pounds."

His sister ran her gaze the length of his lean form. "Doubt it."

Her dry tone made James smile. "I'll have an ice tea." When his sister started to rise, he said, "I can get it."

He saw his mother put a hand on his sister's arm as if to stop her from objecting. James moved stiffly to the refrigerator where he took out the pitcher. He shifted more slowly closer to the cabinet where the glasses where kept. "Do either of you want a glass of tea?"

"I'll have a glass," Abigail said strangely. James flashed her a glance and saw an amused look on her pretty face. She looked so much like their mother, but her hair was blond while his mother's hair was a sandy brown.

"In the cabinet," James teased, filling his own

glass before setting down the pitcher. He felt slightly unsteady as he moved toward the table and pulled out a chair.

"If you sit here, we'll put you to work."

By this time, James was feeling awful. "I think I'll go sit in the other room."

"Don't spill that tea," Abigail taunted with a laugh.

"Brat!" James chuckled as he carefully returned to the great room and took a seat.

A window on the one side of the room was open and faced the driveway. James sat and closed his eyes while wondering what Nell was doing. She had said she would visit again, but it had been four days since he last saw her and he missed her like crazy.

He heard the sound of buggy wheels as a vehicle came down the driveway. *Dat* and Matthew must be back after going to the store to pick up chicken feed and a few other supplies.

He leaned back, closed his eyes. He heard the kitchen screen door slam shut, but he didn't move. Then he sensed someone enter the great room and stare at him. And he knew immediately that it wasn't his father or Matthew.

His eyes flickered open and he thought he was imagining things because he'd wanted so badly to see her. "Nell."

She hesitated in the doorway between the hall and the great room. "James."

"Come in and sit." Then it occurred to him that she might have come for some other reason than to see him. He frowned. "If you have other business and don't have time…"

She came forward and took the chair across from him. "I came to see you."

He couldn't help the grin that burst across his lips. "I'm glad. I've been wanting to see you. Talk with you."

She looked surprised. "You were?"

He picked up his glass. "Would you like some ice tea?"

"That would be nice."

"Abigail!" he shouted. He met Nell's beautiful brown gaze with an amused smile.

"Already got it, *bruder*," Abigail said curtly as she handed Nell a glass. "I don't mind waiting on her."

His sister stayed in the room and hovered.

"Abigail, *danki*. Now please leave us to visit alone," James told her. "I don't need you hovering."

With a sigh of exasperation, his sister left. Nell had a strange look on her face as she stared at him.

"I'm sorry," he said, worrying what Nell was thinking.

"I'm not."

"What?"

"You and your sister…you're just like me and mine."

He released a sigh of relief. "I love her."

"I can tell."

"I love you."

She froze. "What?"

"I said I love you."

She seemed shaken as she looked away. "James, you shouldn't say that. You know I'm marrying John."

"My friend Drew is joining the practice. He's staying."

Nell looked confused. "That's nice. I heard that business is up. You'll need his help."

"Thanks to you." He had learned recently just how much Nell had worked to grow Pierce Veterinary Clinic.

She blushed, looked away.

"Drew is going to be working at the clinic while I work from home."

Nell arched her eyebrows. "You're going to work out of your apartment?"

James gazed at her, watching every nuance of her expression, hoping for a glimpse of her thoughts, something that told him she cared for him more than as a friend. He had told her he loved her, but she hadn't reciprocated. Or did she brush off his feelings because she was Amish and he was English and she was afraid to acknowledge them?

"For a while I'll be living here. *Mam* and *Dat* assured me that it would be all right. Matthew doesn't mind sharing his room for a while." James reflected how his relationship with Matthew had greatly improved since he'd begun to spend time at home.

"You're going to be living here," Nell said. "Why?"

"I'm rejoining the community. I plan to join the church come November."

Nell's mouth opened and closed as if she didn't know what to say.

"I don't understand…"

"If you'd listened to what I said, really listened, you'd know."

Nell stared at the man she loved, unsure of what he was saying. She was afraid to hope, afraid to love, but at the same time, she was terrified of no longer having him in her life.

Now he was telling her that he'd be moving back to the Amish community. Had she only imagined that part because she'd wished for it?

"Nell." He rose from his chair, crossed the distance between them and sat down next to her.

She met his gaze with longing and hope…and

everything she was afraid he'd see in her expression. "Why are you telling me this?"

He took hold of her hand, capturing it between his larger ones. His dark eyes held a sudden intensity that stole her breath. He looked vulnerable with his twin black eyes and bruised face, but she could feel his strength. Dressed in a solid maroon shirt and tri-blend pants held up by black suspenders, James looked as if he had always been Amish, that he'd never left the community. He'd shaved recently, and his firm chin was smooth and drew her attention. What would he look like in a beard as a married man? She gasped as hope reared up, enthralling her.

"James—"

"I love you, Nell. I want to marry you if you'll have me. Will you forget John and become my wife?"

"But, James, you've been *English* for so long."

"That's true. I worked hard to be what I thought my father wanted for me. I went to school, became a veterinarian, worked near a city…and opened a practice here. But you know all that."

Her heart was pounding hard. James was offering her most secret desire—to be his wife, to live with him, have his children…to love him until their lives ended.

"I haven't been happy, Nell, in the *English* world. Not until you stepped through the door of my clinic with Jonas in your arms. You calmed me like you did him. I knew I had to get to know you. I figured right then that I wanted you somehow in my life."

He was running his fingers gently over the back of her hand. His caress tingled and thrilled her.

"Nell," he went on. "I'm happiest here in the community. When I told Adam about my feelings for you—"

She felt a jolt. "You talked with Adam about me?"

His features were apologetic. "I needed his advice. I loved you and thought I didn't have a hope of having you in my life. Adam told me that above everything else, my father wanted me to be happy." He paused, and his hand cupped her face. "That I could easily be a country veterinarian working in our community." He drew a deep breath, released it slowly. "You make me happy. I love you. Please allow me to love you. Marry me."

Tears trickled down her cheeks as she gazed at him. "I said that I'd marry John."

"Does John really want to marry you because you're you? Or because he needs a mother for Nicholas?"

"He wants a mother for Nicholas," she admitted.

"Then it doesn't have to be you. Another woman will do."

She recognized love in his dark eyes. "I'm afraid."

He jerked. "Of me?"

"*Nay*. Of backing out of marrying John, of telling my father of my true feelings." She blinked back tears. "But most of all—what if you aren't happy with being Amish? I want you to be happy," she sobbed. "I don't want you to ever regret the choice you made. I don't want you to be sorry that you married me."

"Sweetheart." He wiped away her tears with his fingers. "I will never regret marrying you. Don't you understand? I love you—so much. Not having you in my life will kill me. You mean that much to me."

"I do?"

He nodded.

"Oh, James, I love you so much it scares me."

"Then you'll marry me?"

"I want to—"

"But?"

"We can wait. I need to know if you change your mind."

"Never! I will never change my mind." He drew her closer. "Nell, let me court you. We have until November before we can marry. Let me prove to you that this life—and you—are what I want more than anything in the world. So, Nell, sweetheart, may I court you?"

Basking in the radiance of his love, Nell felt warm and tingly…and so much in love. *"Ja."*

James groaned, and suddenly he was kissing her, a gentle kiss that made her feel special. He pulled back, his eyes glowing, his mouth curved in a tender smile. "I'm afraid it may be weeks before I can court you properly."

"I can wait."

"But you'll come visit me."

"Ja, James, I'll come," she promised. "Every day."

"And you don't love John."

"Nay, I love you. Always have. Always will.

"And you're going to marry me, not him."

"Ja, I'm going to marry the man I love."

She watched as his eyes closed as she heard him murmur, "Thanks be to *Gott.*"

And Nell had never felt happier. She loved this man, and she would pray every day that God would bless their marriage.

Epilogue

Summer slid into autumn, the months flying by so quickly that Nell wondered where the time had gone. As promised, James had moved all of his things into the Troyer farmhouse. Nell visited him every day while he healed, and afterward, the man spent every moment that they were together proving how much he loved and valued her.

It had been difficult for her to tell her father that she wouldn't be marrying the bishop. Telling the bishop himself had been easier, for as she'd thought, he wasn't done grieving for Catherine. He wasn't ready to marry again.

As for Nicholas, there were plenty of community women who were happy to help with the little boy's care. But as time went by, John kept the boy close with him more often than not.

The fall harvest had come and gone. James had

purchased a small piece of property, and the community had worked during the last months building a home for the soon-to-be-married couple.

The house was perfect, at least to Nell. There was a room for James's satellite veterinary office and plenty of space for the children she and James both hoped to have one day. James asked her to be his veterinary assistant. Nell quickly accepted the position.

Dr. Andrew Brighton was doing well at the clinic. Since Drew would be the only one working in that office, James had insisted that the clinic be renamed to Brighton Animal Hospital, but Drew had disagreed. The friends had compromised by adding Drew's name first to its current name, making it Brighton-Pierce Veterinary Clinic.

Their wedding banns were read in church. James had fit right back into the community, and each passing day had convinced Nell that he truly was happy and belonged.

The morning of their wedding finally arrived. Her parents' house had been transformed to allow for the wedding feast, and the wedding ceremony was at Aunt Katie and Uncle Samuel's.

After riding together while holding hands, Nell and James arrived at the Lapp farm, eager for the services, the ceremony, that would join them as man and wife.

Afterward, they got into the buggy driven by

their attendants—Nell's sister Leah and James's brother, Matthew. Leah and Matthew were chatting about the ceremony, the day and celebration to come.

James leaned closed to Nell, his breath a soft whisper in her ear. "I love you, wife."

Nell smiled as she regarded him with love. "I'll love you forever, husband."

And then her husband of less than an hour leaned close and gave her a tender kiss that stole her breath, her heart—and bound her to him forever. James's head lifted; his dark eyes glowed. His face had healed, and he looked as if he'd never suffered in the accident. Her new husband was easily the most wonderful and handsome man Nell had ever laid eyes on.

She had everything she'd ever wanted—James, the man who loved her, her life's partner. *Thank You, dear Lord, for blessing us with Your love.*

* * * * *

Dear Reader,

Welcome back to the Amish community of Happiness in Lancaster County, Pennsylvania. If you have read any of my Lancaster County Wedding series, you would have met and read about the Lapp brothers, sons of Samuel and Katie Lapp. In *A Secret Amish Love*, Nell Stoltzfus is one of five sisters who are cousins to the Lapp siblings. Although there are still two Lapp brothers who haven't found their true love, I thought them too young to have their own story yet.

Their cousin Nell, on the other hand, is long overdue for marriage. Unfortunately, she finds herself falling for someone she shouldn't. James Pierce, an English veterinarian, is forbidden to her, a young woman who had already joined the Amish church. The fact that James is drawn to her as much as she is to him becomes a problem for the both of them. While her father urges her in one direction, Nell can't keep herself from longing for her forbidden love.

I hope you enjoy Nell's story and your return trip to Amish country in Lancaster County.

Blessing and light,
Rebecca Kertz

Get 2 Free Books,
Plus 2 Free Gifts—
just for trying the Reader Service!

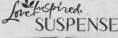

LIS17R2

Get 2 Free Books,
Plus 2 Free Gifts—
just for trying the Reader Service!

HOMETOWN HEARTS ♥

YES! Please send me **The Hometown Hearts Collection** in Larger Print. This collection begins with 3 FREE books and 2 FREE gifts in the first shipment. Along with my 3 free books, I'll also get the next 4 books from the Hometown Hearts Collection, in LARGER PRINT, which I may either return and owe nothing, or keep for the low price of $4.99 U.S./ $5.89 CDN each plus $2.99 for shipping and handling per shipment*. If I decide to continue, about once a month for 8 months I will get 6 or 7 more books, but will only need to pay for 4. That means 2 or 3 books in every shipment will be FREE! If I decide to keep the entire collection, I'll have paid for only 32 books because 19 books are FREE! I understand that accepting the 3 free books and gifts places me under no obligation to buy anything. I can always return a shipment and cancel at any time. My free books and gifts are mine to keep no matter what I decide.

262 HCN 3432 462 HCN 3432

Name	(PLEASE PRINT)	
Address		Apt. #
City	State/Prov.	Zip/Postal Code

Signature (if under 18, a parent or guardian must sign)

Mail to the **Reader Service:**
IN U.S.A.: P.O. Box 1867, Buffalo, NY. 14240-1867
IN CANADA: P.O. Box 609, Fort Erie, Ontario L2A 5X3

* Terms and prices subject to change without notice. Prices do not include applicable taxes. Sales tax applicable in NY. Canadian residents will be charged applicable taxes. This offer is limited to one order per household. All orders subject to approval. Credit or debit balances in a customer's account(s) may be offset by any other outstanding balance owed by or to the customer. Please allow 4 to 6 weeks for delivery. Offer available while quantities last. Offer not available to Quebec residents.

Your Privacy—The Reader Service is committed to protecting your privacy. Our Privacy Policy is available online at www.ReaderService.com or upon request from the Reader Service.

We make a portion of our mailing list available to reputable third parties that offer products we believe may interest you. If you prefer that we not exchange your name with third parties, or if you wish to clarify or modify your communication preferences, please visit us at www.ReaderService.com/consumerschoice or write to us at Reader Service Preference Service, P.O. Box 9062, Buffalo, NY. 14240-9062. Include your complete name and address.

READERSERVICE.COM

Manage your account online!

- Review your order history
- Manage your payments
- Update your address

We've designed the Reader Service website just for you.

Enjoy all the features!

- Discover new series available to you, and read excerpts from any series.
- Respond to mailings and special monthly offers.
- Browse the Bonus Bucks catalog and online-only exculsives.
- Share your feedback.

Visit us at:

ReaderService.com